Heavenfire

JK Allen

also by JK Allen

Angelborn
Heavenfire
Demonkind
Half Blood Alliance

with Carol Allen
The Side of Shadows

Chris, thank you for all your support and for believing my writing is better than I think it is.

Chapter 1

Ginny sighed and looked next to her where Aiden was sleeping easily in the cramped seat of the airplane, despite his long legs. His dark fringe fell over one eye, which would be a striking ice-blue had it been open. Ginny's eyes traced the strong lines in his face, his fluttering lashes, and his full mouth. He looked peaceful. It was the first time she had really seen him so relaxed since their picnic the day before the Council meeting that changed everything. Not just for them, but for every member of the Alliance. The day her father, the angel Grace, made his appearance and had given them their current mission.

Grace had removed two of the leaders of the Alliance Council—Ari's arrogant excuse of a father being one—and put in two new ones, which happily included Jackson. Jackson was not only the chapter head for Lockewood, but was also the man who'd saved and basically raised Aiden after his entire family was killed by demons one night. And Grace had stopped the hearing where Aiden was about to be convicted of being a traitor and kicked out of the Alliance all together. Unfortunately for Ginny, her father had made an appearance to almost everyone but her. But then again, he hadn't seen her in thirteen years, what was another few years to an immortal?

She knew she should be sleeping too, or jet lag would catch up with her, but she had so much on her mind. She huffed, slumping in her seat and gazing out at the patch of pale blue sky outside the window. There was so much uncertainty in her life right now, it was easy to feel overwhelmed. She had no idea if she would ever see her dad, when she would be able to see her mom—who was in hiding—next, when she would even be back in her home, or be able to see her best friend, Pat. Jacob was still after her, and here they were, running off to Bethlehem, trying desperately to foil Jacob's plans before they even knew what they truly were.

She tried to breathe deeply, but the air felt stale and choking, and her anxiety grew rather than abated. The same air that had been inhaled and exhaled by everyone on the plane dozens of times already and recycled was being forced out of the tiny vent above her seat. She wasn't a hundred percent comfortable on airplanes in general, and she was stuck on this one for hours as they made their way to the old world on their secret mission. Somewhere in Bethlehem was a sacred object they had to retrieve—a divine sword that could only be wielded by a human, and that was now going to be entrusted to Aiden's care. It was Aiden's mission as the only human in the Alliance proper. The sword had been passed down from generation to generation, from the first Secret Keeper, one of Aiden's forebears, on down to Aiden. The Keepers were the brother scholars to the Alliance's holy warriors. Unlike the Alliance who were all descended from Grace himself, the Keepers were human, and called that because they kept the knowledge and secrets of the Alliance. The Eternal Tomes, the rituals, sacred locations, and family line of the angel were all records entrusted to them.

It was still so much to process, and she pressed her hands to her stinging eyes. Like the fact that the father she thought was dead was actually Grace, an angel who was very much alive. His mandate was to live on Earth and have children who would assist him in protecting humans from demonkind. They were the Alliance, and she had only just learned of their existence shortly after the night she had almost been kidnapped by a pack of changelings and Jacob.

This also meant that she had powers she barely understood and couldn't control. She also still had yet to see her father.

The worst part of this mission was that Jacob could be anywhere, including right where they were going to be in Bethlehem. Jacob was a powerful half-demon who was determined to get Ginny for his own unknown but surely diabolical plans. All they knew was that he was after the sword to free his father—the first greater demon, Shemi-azaz—from his prison in the deepest pit of Hell. The sword could easily slice through the sacred black chains that kept him there. He was an angel who had sinned greatly—acting as a god, mating with women, and even killing an innocent that he had been charged to protect. Heavenfire had burned him and transformed him into the first demon before he was imprisoned and bound by unbreakable chains. The notion of him getting out was a dangerous prospect—letting the most powerful greater demon free on Earth could never be allowed. There was no telling what evil he would do now that he had nothing to lose. It just couldn't be allowed, and that's why their mission was so crucial. Jacob and his father had to be stopped at all costs.

Once they landed, they'd be staying at the Alliance chapter house in Bethlehem with the three members that lived there regularly. But they weren't able to discuss why they were there. The mission was given on a need-to-know only basis. Even their friends back home didn't know where they were or what they were doing. Only Jackson knew. It was nerve wracking for Ginny. To be suddenly thrust among and dependent upon strangers halfway across the world while keeping such a big secret from them. And Jacob was searching for the same sword. It was a huge risk that they might be in the same location as him, and all while he was so desperate to get to Ginny. He had tried to kidnap her, then her mom. And he had succeeded in getting his hands on her best friend, Pat, trying to use him as a bargaining chip for her surrender. She and Aiden had managed to save him, but no one knew what Jacob was truly capable of or willing to do to get to her. She let out a breath, trying to calm her nerves. *This would work out fine; it had to.*

She went back to reading to calm herself. She could

do this, and she wasn't alone. She had Aiden. This thought made her smile. The captain announced they were nearing approach, and Aiden stirred next to her. He gave her a crooked grin as he rubbed the sleep out of his eyes. Her mouth went dry as the plane began its descent. She could hardly believe she was in another part of the world, in another country. Her heart pounded as the wheels touched down. She had never been this far from home before. Her shoulders ached as they tightened and her hands clenched into fists.

They landed and went through customs, which took hours and strained her nerves even more. She was nervous about answering their questions wrong and about how long the whole process was taking. They gathered their bags and walked outside the terminal where a tall, stern looking, young man was holding a sign with their names on it. He had short brown hair, deep set brown eyes, and a strong nose. Ginny swallowed hard as they approached him. They had already grabbed their bags, and Ginny felt like she was taking halting steps towards him. She wished he would smile as he eyed them. The crowds around her seemed to swell as she followed Aiden.

"That's us," Aiden said, striving to sound casual. The man was definitely intimidating.

"I am Ezra. I am here to taxi you back to the house. I hope you had a pleasant trip." His voice was low and calm as he spoke. He held a solemnity about him that seemed to characterize him in his actions and choice of words.

"It was great," Ginny said and was rewarded with Ezra's first, small smile. It was amazing what a difference it made, softening him and easing some of her trepidation.

"Follow me," he said, grabbing Ginny's luggage from her. Aiden trailed after them out to the car. Ginny was surprised to see so many American cars on the narrow, twisting streets that surrounded the airport. But then again, Motor City was as American as it got, and it made sense others would drive American makes abroad. The streets were crowded and chaotic as the cars weaved through each other, everyone in a rush to drop off or pick up passengers. As they pulled into town, they saw the buildings stacked on either side, looking nothing like home.

"How was the flight?" Ezra asked again as they pulled out of the airport.

"Uneventful. Which is a good thing," Ginny answered, leaning out the window to take in the sights now that they were actually in the new city.

"Didn't notice. I slept the whole ride," Aiden said from the back seat.

"You didn't sleep?" Ezra turned to look at Ginny, brow creased.

"I was too nervous. It was my first time flying overseas," she admitted with an embarrassed grin.

He nodded and returned his gaze to the road. Tall stone buildings hunched on either side of the street, and Ginny was glad she didn't have to drive down these narrow, winding roads. Many of the women she saw walking along the street had their hair covered. Ginny ran a hand through her own brown hair, feeling self conscious. How much would she stand out here amongst the hijabs, headscarves, and modest dress? She hoped fervently that she would not stand out too much. Though it seemed unlikely she wouldn't, and her breath caught in her throat. She hadn't even thought of what clothes to wear that would be appropriate to the culture here, just that it was the end of summer, turning autumn in the desert. She had to stifle a groan.

"What brings you to Bethlehem?" Ezra asked in a calculated way. He gave Ginny a pointed glance she didn't know how to respond to.

"An important mission," Aiden answered from the backseat, not skipping a beat. "We hope it's not an inconvenience to you."

"Of course not. Can you share your mission with us?"

"Sorry, no. The angel gave it to us himself, and we were told to keep it secret due to its significance."

Ezra nodded, but frowned, making Ginny squirm uneasily in her seat. Already they were getting questions they had to answer carefully. It didn't sit well with her at all. Keeping secrets. She just hoped she wouldn't have to lie to anyone about anything. She was awful at it, and did not want to get any practice at getting better.

"You are welcome with us to be sure," Ezra responded in the same monotonous tone he had used this whole time.

"Thanks, we are grateful for your hospitality," Ginny rushed to say, not wanting him to add more to that.

They had to stop through several checkpoints to get to the residence. Ezra didn't seem ruffled at all, but Ginny was on edge each time they slowed, her passport clutched in her hands, ready to hand over. Worried about the officer's questions and answering them wrong.

"We are almost there. You will like the house, I think." Ezra smiled again and Ginny settled down in her seat, thankful the checkpoints were over and done with.

They turned off the main road onto a narrow street. These houses were spaced farther apart, and they pulled up to a picturesque manor with an olive grove settled behind it. It was a two-storey tan structure.

"Welcome home," Ezra said as he parked.

Ginny unbuckled herself. "It's beautiful."

Ezra's voice swelled with pride. "The best part is the grove. Peaceful and full of savory air to breathe. It is a pleasure to spend many an afternoon there."

They all climbed out of the car, grabbing their luggage from the trunk. Ginny's bag was new to her—Jackson had bought it for her, and it still didn't feel like hers, but at least she'd been allowed home to collect her clothes and personal belongings. The two of them followed Ezra up to the house where a gorgeous girl in her twenties opened the door.

"Welcome." She embraced them one-by-one, her brown curls bouncing. She had warm, hazel eyes that caught the light beautifully and a brilliant smile. "I am Sarai. Welcome to our home, brother and sister."

"Thanks for having us." Ginny smiled brightly.

Sarai laughed, then remembered herself. "Please come in. You must be tired. There is tea, then you will rest."

They entered, and set their luggage in the hallway next to the stairs that led to the bedrooms. Then they sat down at a table in the kitchen. It had a white, lace tablecloth draped over it with two candles in holders placed in the center. Sarai poured steaming tea from a silver tea kettle into cups that Ezra then placed in front of them.

"Thank you." Ginny picked up her cup and blew on the tea. The smell of mint filled her nostrils.

"Are you hungry?" Sarai asked, walking to the fridge.

"A bit," Aiden said sheepishly.

Sarai made a tray with hummus, pita, olives, and some fresh vegetables. Ezra carried it to Aiden with a smile.

A middle-aged, portly man strode into the room from the other side of the hall. "Ah, you've arrived. I am Asa, head of this chapter, and I welcome you here."

"Nice to meet you," Aiden said between bites.

"Slow down," Asa said with a laugh. "You Americans do everything too fast, even eating. But life is about enjoying each moment. Savoring it. Here there is no rush. No need for speed."

Aiden blushed, then swallowed.

"You could learn a lot from us," Asa said gravely, before walking out into the olive grove. Two large french doors opened out into the grove, displaying the rows of green trees that stretched in neat lines from the house.

Ginny had a few uncharitable thoughts about Asa, and wasn't sad to see him leave so quickly.

"It is our favorite place. To sit in the sun, smelling the plants and letting your thoughts unravel," Ezra explained, looking out the door with a soft smile on his face.

"It's a great place to think and relax. We often spend our afternoons there," Sarai added.

Ginny sighed, feeling overwhelmed and homesick. "I'm sure it's lovely."

Sarai made a face. "Are you being sarcastic?"

"No, not at all." Ginny's cheeks flushed. *Had she said the wrong thing?*

Sarai threw her hand on her hip and glared at Ginny as if she was a misbehaving child. "We do not like sarcasm in this house. Maybe you are new to the Alliance, but we who have grown up in it understand that each member must speak respectfully to those who are our seniors. Never sarcastically."

"I wasn't being sarcastic." Ginny tried to reassure her, but could tell the older woman didn't believe her. *And why bring up she wasn't raised in the Alliance? Or that Sarai was older.* Ginny hated when people demanded respect because of when they happened to be born, and not because they'd earned it. Especially since they so rarely reciprocated it.

Sarai rolled her eyes and Ginny's jaw clenched at the hypocrisy of it. Instead of letting her temper get to her, she set down her cup and stood. "I'd like some sleep, if you'd be so kind as to show me where my room is."

"I will take you there." Ezra walked to the stairs, picking up her luggage and leading her up them. "You're here," he said as they reached a bedroom off the landing.

Her room was near a bathroom she noted with relief.

"And you are our guest. If you need anything, do not hesitate to ask."

Ginny didn't have to fake this smile, and Ezra returned it. "Thanks. For making me feel so welcomed." She waved at him as she stepped inside and closed the door quietly.

She dragged her luggage to the corner by the wardrobe and kicked off her shoes. Running her fingers through her hair, she took a look around her. The room was comfortable and homey with a quilt draped over the bed and knickknacks on the wooden desk.

Ginny was exhausted and their mission was only just starting. She needed a nap, wishing she had gotten some sleep on the plane. It was only afternoon here, but she would need time to adjust to this new time zone. She plopped right on top of the quilt, shoving the pillow under her head. She thought of her father. She still hadn't seen him. *Would she ever?* Tears sprang to her eyes. Even Aiden had seen him. Even Jackson. Sure it had been on official business as Aiden liked to remind her, but she couldn't help but ask herself why she wasn't worth the time? A tear spilled down her cheek, but she was too tired to wipe it away. Her father wasn't dead, but he was still just as far away from her as ever. She rolled over, her hand clenching into a fist, and closed her eyes. Luckily, sleep came to her quickly.

Chapter 2

Aiden looked over the directions to the temple he had gotten from Jackson before they had left on their mission as the bus ticked down the road. They had planned to get the sword as soon as they could slip away, but needed to know how to reach it safely, being foreigners. He and Ginny had snuck out this afternoon to complete their mission when Asa and the others weren't looking. Ginny had slept through the night, then they had a pleasant enough morning, having a hearty breakfast and joining in training with Ezra and Sarai. Ginny had studiously not said anything to Sarai unless prompted. They both thought it was better to try and hold the peace, which apparently meant Ginny not interacting with Sarai. She had even ranted about the "little American brat" after Ginny had gone to rest the day before. Aiden defended Ginny, but quickly left the situation. Sarai seemed to hold a grudge against Ginny, so there was nothing to do but ignore her. It was ugly behavior, and Aiden wanted nothing to do with it.

The members seemed to be watching them closely though, until the afternoon, when the Bethlehem members had gone outside to be in the grove again, enjoying tea. Aiden and Ginny slipped out the front door and down the street towards the bus stop Aiden had seen on their way in before the other members noticed. Ginny and Aiden were on their way to retrieve the sword, named Usurper, before Jacob could get his hands on it.

"I hate the name Usurper," Aiden muttered to Ginny, whose leg was bouncing up and down in the seat next to him.

She turned, a red glint in her chocolate brown hair as she looked at him pensively. "Why's that?"

"Usurper is another name for Jacob. In the Bible, he stole his brother's birthright. And Jacob's the last person we want to get their hands on it. It shouldn't be named after him. Or rather, he shouldn't be named for it."

"I hadn't thought of that. Why don't you just rename it?"

It was such an innocent question, but it hadn't even occurred to him that it was a possibility. He thought hard about a new name.

"Well, Jacob's trying to do a lot of bad things to the Alliance, and we want to use it against him. What about Redeemer?"

She looked at him and smiled, gold flecks swimming in her brown eyes. "I like it. We should call it that from now on."

He smiled, almost missing their stop. He leaned over to pull the cord, letting the driver know to stop for them. Standing as the bus slowed to a jerking halt, they made their way forward and disembarked into the cool afternoon air. Autumn was arriving, though it was very different in this part of the world. He was used to Lockewood, where the trees would be starting to change into brilliant tones of yellow and red and the air would hold a crispness to it.

The buildings around them were all made of stone and clay, with low stooping doorways that opened out onto the narrow streets. People walked around, taking their time as they went about their day. Asa was right about there not being as much of a rush here. He paused for a moment to take in their surroundings and make sure no one suspicious was paying attention to them.

The sun glinted in his eyes, and he raised his hand to

block out the rays. Shopkeepers swept their doorways of the sand that had accumulated, but no one was watching them beyond the few stares of curiosity they got as obvious visitors to the area. He felt the slight thrill that came from being in a new city in a new country and smiled at Ginny.

This was an adventure, and even though he was nervous about getting the sword, he was happy to be experiencing something new and exciting for once. And this was also something only he could do for the Alliance. He had spent the last seven years devoting himself to the Alliance and their cause. Living it in every sense of the word and working hard to be a good member the others could rely on. But he was human, and therefore, always lacking and an outcast. But this was his birthright. This sword was guarded by his family for countless generations. And now it was up to him to retrieve it and keep it safe. His chest swelled at the thought.

The temple where they were headed was built into the wall that surrounded it, with a low door he had to stoop to enter. It had a wider walkway than the rest of the street, apparently to accommodate the daily worshippers. The temple was daubed and darker in some spots where more had been smeared than other places. Everything smelled musty from all the sand that swirled at their feet, but Aiden breathed in deeply in spite of it.

"Are you sure this is the right place?" Ginny asked in a hushed voice as they entered the alcove. It was lit by candelabras which filled the interior with a soft, golden glow.

"The coordinates on my family ring match and it's a temple," Aiden said with a shrug. To be honest, he didn't really know how this worked. Only that he would need to present the key his mother had given him and his signet ring that marked him as a King. He also kept his voice low, not just to keep their words from the other people scattered around the temple, but the weight and feel of the place seemed to demand reverent respect from them.

"Welcome," a pleasant looking man in long robes said as he approached them. "May I assist you?" He blinked from behind round glasses and smiled at them wanly.

Praying that the man would understand what was

happening, Aiden pulled off his necklace that held a key and ring, holding the key up.

"Ah, that is an old key. Not often seen here. Please, follow me, honored guests." There wasn't even a hint of surprise in his voice, and Aiden wondered for a moment how many times the man had dealt with similar situations.

They walked behind him as he leisurely strolled deeper into the temple. Aiden worked not to step on him as they paced behind him, past the lit candles and praying figures to a back room where they found themselves alone. It was similarly lit by candelabras, which flickered in the shadows in the corners of the room. His mind was racing. Here was something that had tied his family together. Their need to protect this secret for the Alliance. This place was full of secrets, his family's included. He breathed faster at the thought.

"May I?" The man held out his hand.

Aiden placed the ring and key into his outstretched hand with some reticence and cleared his throat.

"Please wait here." He left the room without another word.

Aiden gave Ginny a sideways look. *Would this work?*

"At least he knew what the key meant. I was worried we'd have to explain everything and look like idiots," she said, echoing his own internal worry from the start.

"Yeah," he said with a grin. "We're here for a magic sword because an angel told us to get it for him, so we can save the world from an evil half-demon bent on world domination."

They laughed at how absurd that would sound to most people, then hushed each other as their laughs echoed through the cave-like room. After a few minutes, the man returned, carrying something long, swathed in black cloth, and a worn guitar case.

"I believe this is yours, young sir," he said with a mischievous grin.

The man held out his necklace next, the key and ring hanging down like a pendulum. Aiden put it back around his neck, comforted by its familiar weight against his chest. Aiden took the cloth covered package from him next. He unwrapped the cloth to find a gleaming sword with a dark luster to it and a silver hilt. The hilt was engraved with different sigils in the angelic tongue that prevented it from being wielded by angelborn or demonkind alike. They did not react to his touch at all.

"I trust this is what you sought?" The man inclined his head at the sword Aiden was holding.

Aiden nodded. "Yes."

"Then, I only offer you this." The man held out the guitar case. "As a means of transport. Not many carry around a sword these days. And I assume you would like to keep it from being confiscated by an overzealous police officer." He flashed white teeth at them.

Aiden crouched down and placed the sword inside the case and pulled off his scribe. Their scribes were what they used to write sigils in the Angelic Tongue that worked like magic. It had always reminded him of those cigarette holders women smoked out of in the roaring twenties, but shortened and tipped with a golden, chalk-like substance. Jackson had taught him the specific sigil to use for this. One that would keep others from opening the case without his permission. He wasn't angelborn, but the sigils did work for him if he concentrated, just not as strongly as they would for say Ginny or even Tali. But he hoped it would be enough to keep the sword safe until they got home.

It was the best they could do. Ginny had never written a sigil before, and they had decided now wasn't the time to start. This was too important, and she was as of yet untested. Sigils would undoubtedly work for her, but she didn't really know any.

Concentrating on nothing but the sigil, he marked the case and prayed that it would work before standing back up.

"Thanks," he said to the man. "We'll see ourselves out." He didn't have the patience to walk behind him again.

"Feel free to light a candle on your way out." And with one last smile, he turned and left them.

Aiden led them back to the chapel and was about to walk out when Ginny put a hand on his arm. "I want to light a candle," she said, turning red.

"Of course. I'll light one too. For my family."

He swallowed past the lump in his throat as they turned and walked into the alcove. Aiden spent a few quiet minutes staring at the flickering flames of the tall white candles at the back wall. They were surrounded by worshippers praying, their lips moving in silence as they clasped their hands together. He thought of his lost family, his twin sisters' laughter as they played, his mother's soft smile as she kissed him good morning, his father reading with his glasses perched on his head, lounging in his favorite chair in the evenings. It had been seven years since he had seen them, but they were never far from his thoughts. Memories he cherished from their lives before they had been ripped apart by demons in the night were all he had left. He hoped they were in a better place now. He wondered what Ginny was thinking as she stared into the flame of her tall white candle, a fervent look on her face.

They caught the bus back to the chapter house in silence. They had gotten what they came for, but now they had to keep it safe, which was no easy prospect.

Ezra met them at the door, a stern look on his usually serious face.

"You went somewhere without me," he said, crossing his arms. At six-foot-four, Ezra took up most of the doorway. *It wasn't as if they had orders to have a chaperone at all times.* Aiden rankled at the thought.

"We were fine," Ginny said brightly. "Just a quick trip into town."

"You shouldn't have gone without me. It is dangerous for you two. You are strangers here, and you could have gotten lost, or worse. Heaven forbid." His brow furrowed as he signed the cross over himself, glaring at Ginny smiling back at him.

"But we didn't. Now are you going to let us in? I'd really love a glass of water."

He still scowled, but said, "Let me get it for you."

They followed Ezra inside the house, which was quiet. Aiden was used to more than three people living in their chapter house, so the quiet was a little unsettling here.

"I didn't know you played," Ezra said as they reached the stairs, glancing at the guitar case.

"Trying to learn and found a great deal on one. I don't play yet, but now I can learn," Aiden said as he slipped up the stairs and hid the case under his bed. He straightened the bed covers to keep it out of direct sight, then he went back downstairs to join Ginny and Ezra in the kitchen.

"How did you like the city?" Ezra asked, handing her the glass of water.

"I like it! And I love hearing a new language. It's so beautiful," Ginny answered, sitting down.

"Well, you should learn it."

"The Angelic Tongue is all I can handle learning at the moment. It's still like Latin to me."

Everyone in the Alliance used the Angelic Tongue for all their sigils and even some chants. Ginny had barely had any lessons in anything Alliance related before they had gotten their mission. Aiden would be surprised if she could recognize more than one or two sigils. It was an unearthly language, literally, so there was nothing comparable to make it easier to learn.

Aiden sat next to her at the table. "I had a hard time learning when I first joined."

Ezra chuckled. "I started learning as a toddler. My father insisted on it."

Ginny sighed, pushing her bangs out of her face. "I'm afraid I'm too old to learn the Angelic Tongue."

"You're only sixteen." Aiden poked her side. He didn't want Ginny to think too much about when she was a toddler. At that age, she was told her father, the angel, had died when nothing could have been further from the truth. She had spent most of her life mourning his loss before learning the truth, very recently.

She laughed. "That's six years later than you. My brain is too set in its ways now."

"And where have you two been?" Asa said, striding into the room. He looked annoyed as he stared at them, and Ginny stopped laughing.

"Just out, seeing the city," Aiden answered gruffly. He wasn't inclined to tell Asa anything, let alone about Redeemer or that they had completed the first part of their mission already.

Asa gave him a pointed look. "You should have told us where you were going." His lips pursed.

"Sorry," Ginny chimed in. "We didn't want to bother anyone."

"It's no bother," Asa said, forcing a smile. "But we do worry about you. So far from home. And you are here for a reason."

"We are." Aiden met his gaze, refusing to blink first.

"We wish you would share that reason...."

Aiden sat up stiffly. "Sorry, that we can't do. Which reminds me, I have to call Jackson. Excuse me."

Aiden made his way up to his room, then waited at the door to make sure no one had followed him. When he was reassured by their voices continuing in the kitchen, he dialed Jackson's number on the cell phone he had gotten from Ezra last night to use while they were there. He had already checked it for bugs or apps to record his activity.

"Aiden, do you have any news for me?" Jackson cut to the point.

"Yes, we have Redeemer."

"Redeemer?" The question was clear in his voice.

"I renamed Usurper. So it's not named after Jacob, and so no one will know we're talking about it."

"That is smart thinking," Jackson said without missing a beat.

Aiden smiled, pleased with himself.

"Was it hard to get? Do the others know?"

Aiden pushed his bangs out of his eyes. "No, Ginny and I snuck out when no one was looking. Asa keeps asking why we're here though. He and Ezra are insisting we don't go anywhere without them."

"He was told it was to be a secret at all costs."

Aiden rolled his eyes. "Well, that doesn't seem to sit well with him. He just asked us again before I called."

Jackson paused. "I will have a word with him."

"I don't like the looks of him," Aiden found himself saying.

Jackson sounded surprised. "You do not trust him? He has been the chapter head there for many years."

"I know, it's just a gut feeling I have and the way he's

being so nosy.”

He hesitated again. “Well, do not reveal anything. The mission is too important.”

“You can count on me.”

“I know,” he said gravely. “And I have another mission for you.”

Aiden perked up. “What’s that?”

“I discovered that Jacob is after the Eternal Tomes while at the Keeper’s house. The Keeper had left letters hidden in a false panel in the wall. One of them detailed Jacob’s agenda to get the tomes. The second tome is in Bethlehem. You must retrieve it immediately. Before Jacob discovers it.”

Aiden ran a hand through his hair. “What does he want with the books?”

“To use them. There are powerful sigils and rituals in them. He must not succeed, Aiden.”

“Understood. I’ll tell Ginny right away.”

“In this case, you will have to consult Asa. I have no way of knowing where the Secret Keeper resides without his knowledge. Asa will have to take you there. But this mission need not be as secret. All of the Alliance must work together to protect the tomes.”

“I’ll tell them right now.”

“You need not mention Jacob directly, unless necessary. Just that you must see the Keeper. Stay safe, Aiden. Keep Ginny safe too.”

“I will.”

Aiden disconnected and ran down the stairs to the front room, where Asa sat with Ezra and Ginny. Ginny looked uncomfortable, perched next to Asa on the couch. He was looking at her sternly while Ezra watched them both from across the room with an inscrutable look on his face.

“Asa, we must go to the Secret Keeper at once.”

Asa gave him a cold look. “Of what do you speak?”

“Jackson had given me orders to check in with the Secret Keeper here. He said you would know where to find him, and that I could let you know about our mission now that we are here in person and can speak face-to-face.”

“What is your mission?” Ezra asked dryly.

"We need the tomes."

"What are those again?" Ginny asked, turning to face Aiden.

"Three books given to the Alliance by the angel Grace. They contain important sigils and rituals."

"We cannot today," Asa said with a frown.

"But it's important," Ginny interrupted. "Jackson said we needed to go for a reason."

Asa held up his hands. "We can go another time, I am sure."

"But...." Aiden began.

"No buts. I cannot go today. It will wait."

"You could just tell us where it is," Ginny suggested.

"No, and the matter is final." And with that he walked out of the room. throwing his hands up in annoyance as he went.

"We will go tomorrow," Ezra reassured them, but Aiden was seething. This was too important to put off. He hadn't mentioned Jacob, but still, even without that information, this wasn't something to be put off.

How could Asa not understand what was at stake here? He clenched his jaw at the thought. Asa was being stupid and the risk was too high to be borne. How could he just sit here when Jacob might be after the tome this very instant?

Ginny put a hand on his arm. "Let's take a walk in the grove."

He nodded and followed her out without a word.

"What did Jackson say exactly?" Ginny turned to ask him once they were alone in the grove. The trees all stood in quiet lines, dark green leaves fluttering in the wind. It was the last of their season, but for now everything was still peaceful and vibrant. Aiden felt his head clearing as he breathed in the earthy scent of the soil.

"He said Jacob was after the tomes. He found a letter in the Keeper's house. That means the two remaining Secret Keepers are in danger, and so are the tomes."

Ginny sighed. "These tomes sound important."

They walked deeper into the trees and Aiden glanced behind him. There was no sign anyone from the house was following them.

"They are. They contain much of our knowledge, and they would be dangerous in Jacob's hands. These are sigils even most of the Alliance doesn't know. Ones only known to the Secret Keepers and the angel. Deemed too powerful for us to use, in case they tempt us to stray."

Ginny shook her head. "I can't believe Asa wouldn't take us today to secure those."

Aiden's fists curled. "He has no good reason not to. I don't know what he's up to, but we go first thing tomorrow."

Ginny nodded, brushing the hair from his eyes with a soft touch. He wanted to reach out to her, to pull her close and feel reassurance that everything was going to be alright. That they would save the tomes and stop Jacob once and for all. But this wasn't the time to be childish.

Ginny brushed his hand with hers. "We'll save the tomes."

"We have to."

Ginny hooked her arm around Aiden's, and they continued their stroll through the grove, talking of happier things.

Chapter 3

Ginny woke up early to go to the Keeper's house. A cool breeze blew in through her window, filling her room with the natural scent of the recently watered grove. It didn't smell particularly of olives, which surprised her. But more of the trees and the leaves and the dirt they grew in. It was a pleasant way to start the day. *If only today were pleasant.*

She showered quickly and got ready, full of nervous energy. After all, Jacob was after the same thing they were, and who knew where in the world he was at the moment. He could even be there in the same town now. She shivered at the thought.

Drying and braiding her hair down her back, she smiled anxiously at her reflection. Her eyes were a somber brown, her face serious. She shook her head to clear it and got up. It was time to find Aiden.

Knocking on Aiden's door, a knot formed in her stomach and a sinking feeling filled her. She tried to ignore it and smiled when Aiden answered the door, already fully dressed.

"Let's go get that tome," he said, zipping up his hoodie.

They made their way down to the kitchen for some

coffee and to look for Asa. He was already there, making eggs. Next to him on the counter were some breakfast meats and tea.

"Good morning, breakfast will be ready shortly," he said too brightly.

"We really should get to the Keeper's house," Aiden said, pouring a cup of aromatic coffee. He handed it to Ginny who took a sip, before pouring one of his own.

"Breakfast is important," Asa chided, plating the eggs.

Aiden rolled his eyes at Ginny, but kept his mouth shut.

"Aiden's right," Ginny began. "This is really important. We have to get there. We need to leave now." She put her cup down on the counter and gave him a pleading look.

Asa frowned. "I am not going without breakfast. You are both in too much of a hurry."

"Then tell us where it is and we'll go ourselves," Aiden said, putting down his cup and sloshing coffee onto his hand. He reached for a napkin, silently cursing.

Asa shook his head and frowned. "That is dangerous. You should not go out in the city alone."

"We're equipped to handle it. We are Alliance, after all," Aiden insisted.

Asa studied them for a moment, then smiled. "It is on a trail on Mt. Hermon," he said. Then he gave them directions and placed the pan in the sink. Ginny couldn't shake the unease she felt as Aiden took down the instructions on his phone.

They left in a huff and the knot in Ginny's stomach grew. Once again they were on their own, walking into an unknown situation where Jacob could be waiting anywhere.

"Maybe we should go with Ezra," she said as they walked towards the bus stop. The sun was pale in the light colored sky. Everything was washed out and unfamiliar.

Aiden sped up his steps and Ginny rushed to keep up. "There's no time to wait. We should have done this yesterday."

"I know. And you're not wrong, but this doesn't feel right."

He sighed. "You're worried about Jacob, aren't you?"

"Well, I can't control my powers yet. If we run into him, I don't know that I can help you for sure." She bit her lip.

He shrugged. "I've got my knives. I'm not worried about him."

Ginny nodded and swallowed. She worried. Jacob wasn't something to be taken lightly. They had to get to the Keeper before he did.

"Does this Keeper live in a church at least?" she asked, flipping her braid behind her. Once again she noticed the way most of the women around them covered their hair. Some Keepers lived in churches because the blessed grounds protected them from demons.

"No, I don't think so," he replied, rubbing his neck while the bus lurched to a stop in front of them.

They got on and Ginny sat upright and still next to Aiden, trying to take up as little space as possible. She couldn't shake her nerves, palms clammy and leg bouncing up and down. The sounds of people talking around her, which the day before had sounded lilting and musical, just made her feel left out and excluded. She was a stranger in this part of the world, and she felt it keenly now. It felt like everyone was staring at them and whispering.

"Our stop," Aiden leaned over to say in her ear. He leaned over to pull the cord, and they both rose, Ginny clutching at the hem of her shirt as the bus swayed to a stop.

They got off, the sun traveling higher in the sky above them. They had to walk a while to get to the trail leading up the mountain. Ginny wiped the sweat from her brow. Now that they were out in the morning sun and walking, she was warm. Aiden had told her Mt. Hermon was where the Burned Ones had made their promise to disobey God, which had led to them being chained in the pits of perdition. She recalled the transformation of Shemiazaz from the blond glory of the angel to the scaled grey form of the first greater demon. His black talons that raked against the stone walls that trapped him. The ebony chains of darkness that snaked around his neck and waist. Shaking the mental picture of the greater demon away, she focused on what was in front of her instead. The trail wound along before they saw a mile marker sign, marked with what looked like butterfly wings. The marker indicated it was two miles away.

"That's the one," Aiden said pointing at the wings. "That's the symbol for the Secret Keeper's house. I've seen it in class before."

"At least we found the right trail," she said, looking up at the cloud strewn sky.

Tan dust swirled around their feet. The ground itself held an orange hue that was completely new to Ginny. Back home the dirt was a dark brown or black. Here and there, sparse trees dotted the landscape, gnarled and stunted. Again, the foreignness of the moment struck Ginny, and she felt alien here. She watched Aiden's back as he trudged up the trail.

"I think we're almost there," he said, turning.

They crested a plateau and the Keeper's house came into view. It was a simple two-storey building, and Ginny watched in horror as Jacob casually walked right out the front door. Her heart leapt into her throat.

"Aiden," she called out.

Jacob stopped at her cry, shouldering the black bag in his hand as if he hadn't a care in the world. He stood tall and proud, his black hair falling into his steel grey eyes. His strong jaw was set as he gave them a crooked smile, and he pulled out a black dagger with a low luster. Even Ginny knew that meant it was a demon blade, made of metal poisonous to humans and angelborn. Aiden grabbed a knife of his own and ran up to meet Jacob. Jacob swung first, hand snaking out in a wide arc about chest high. Aiden jumped back, planting his feet before he darted in again. Jacob aimed his next swing at Aiden's neck, nicking his chin with his blade. Ginny sucked in a breath. What was she doing? She had no weapons, but she didn't need weapons. Her blood and her birthright were her weapons. All she had to do was summon the Spirit or heavenfire. That was stronger than any other weapon.

She wrinkled her nose and tried to concentrate, but her heart was pounding and beads of sweat were trailing down her neck, distracting her. She still did not know how to control her powers. They had been triggered by extreme situations before, when her mom was in danger and when Aiden was dying in that warehouse. The thought of Aiden covered in blood as he fell to his knees still haunted her. But it made her more hesitant than confident. If she didn't do it this time, that was how things could end here.

Jacob brought his knife down hard, and Aiden blocked it with his forearm at Jacob's wrist. But Aiden was sweating and breathing heavily already. He flung Jacob backwards and went on the attack. Jacob blocked and dodged, a twisted smile on his face. Aiden was doing his best, and his training served him well, but he was slowing down in his movements. The poison was starting to take effect from his cut. He swung wide and Jacob dodged and moved in closer.

Ginny shuddered, trying to get control of herself. She closed her eyes, breathing fast and shallow, she tried to focus on what she had felt the first time she called up her powers. But she had to make sure Aiden was okay, and her eyes fluttered open. Just in time to see Aiden and Jacob grappling. Aiden lost his grip on his knife and Ginny panicked.

"Stop!" she screamed, running towards them with her hands out in front of her. Jacob flinched, backing away from them both quickly. He had seen her wield heavenfire and destroy dozens of changelings in minutes when they had rescued Pat. He held his knife out towards her, side stepping away, then fled down the path.

Aiden lurched after him, but Ginny placed her hands on his shoulders to stop him.

"Let me heal you." *Would she be able to?* She had never used a sigil before and doubted whether she could do it right. It had never really even been explained to her. *I have to try.*

"We have to stop him," Aiden huffed, trembling.

"It was a demon blade. Look at you, you're already sick from it. Now let me heal you."

She pulled her scribe over her head and tried to recall the healing sigil, picturing it in her mind. "I just have to concentrate on the sigil, right?" she asked, hand poised. She'd never done this before, and her hand shook with the pressure of the moment.

"Yeah, but you have to stay still to do it." Aiden's voice was shaky.

"I am standing still, you're just dizzy. Come here." She grabbed his hand and carefully drew the sigil. The sigils were words written in the Angelic Tongue that worked like magic as far as Ginny could tell. She had seen Tali use a sigil to protect Pat after they had saved him from Jacob. She had seemed to be praying first, so Ginny had followed suit, mouthing a quick plea as she wrote.

Aiden shook his hand and took a deep breath.

"How are you feeling?"

"I'm fine. Now let's go stop Jacob."

"He has a sigil that lets him travel anywhere in the world in a second. Remember how he disappeared at the factory? He's long gone by now."

"So what do we do?"

"Oh my gosh, the Keeper," she exclaimed in a rush.

"Let's go."

They rushed into the house. There were clear signs of a struggle. The furniture was in disarray, with chairs toppled over and a table pushed out of the way. It was dark in the house and suffocating. The furniture was simple and some of it was broken. Keepers weren't rich and could often afford few luxuries from what she had noticed. But this was even more sparse than that. She scanned the room for signs of life.

"Hello?" Aiden called out into the silence.

"Do you think he's okay?" Ginny asked shakily.

"Help me," a weak voice called out from upstairs.

They ran towards the sound and found an older man sprawled on the floor of what looked to be a study. Blood stained the shirt at his stomach and his breathing was ragged. His face was pale and covered in beads of sweat.

"He needs a healing sigil," Aiden said to Ginny, who gripped her scribe again in her clammy hand. This was much more serious than Aiden's wound had been. Could she do this? He unbuttoned the man's shirt, exposing a nasty wound with demon poisoning twisting outwards, like swirling vines of black.

Ginny focused on the sigil, then wrote it as clearly as she could on the Keeper's chest, praying it would work. It flashed gold once, then sank into his skin. He sighed and Ginny watched as the marks of poison vanished and the skin stitched itself together again. With the small nick on Aiden it hadn't been as noticeable, now she could watch as the long deep gash filled in with healthy pink flesh and color returned to his skin.

"Thank you," the man sobbed, his voice already stronger. He was older, with curling silver hair and crow's feet around his hazel eyes. But he was lean and looked strong for his age. His eyes shone with tears as he looked at them.

"It's all my fault. We were warned, but no one would do anything. And now he has taken the Book of Rituals. That demonspawn. What will we do? It was Jacob, right?"

"It was. And for now we go back to the chapter house and figure out how to get it back," Aiden said emphatically.

The man sighed. "What is your name, son?"

"Aiden. And this is Ginny. We're from the Lockewood chapter of the Alliance in America."

"I am Elisha, and I will go with you." He made a sour face at the thought, but allowed Aiden to help him to his feet. "I must speak to Asa and figure this out."

Ginny turned to leave, but kicked something on the floor. It made a tinkling sound as it rolled down the hallway. Aiden picked it up with a strange look on his face.

"This is …."

Ginny peered at it. "Oh, it's Jacob's ring," she answered.

"What do you mean it's Jacob's ring?"

"The one he always wears on his pinky," she explained as Aiden's face paled. It was stamped with the letter K, surrounded by a crown. "He must have dropped it."

Elisha brushed past them, running a shaky hand through his mussed hair. *Was he really okay?* He seemed to be walking steadily as he walked into another room. Ginny watched him closely, looking for signs her sigil hadn't worked.

"That can't be his ring." Aiden's voice interrupted her

thoughts. He looked at her, a pained expression on his face. He regarded her for a long moment. "Never mind." He shook his head and gave her a small smile, but he was pale and his face was drawn with worry.

"Are you okay? Does this ring mean something?"

"No. It's nothing." *Why was he looking at her like that?*

"If you two are ready," Elisha began. He had changed his shirt and came out of a door buttoning it. At least his color was returning to his face now, Ginny noted with a small smile.

"Let's get back to the house," Aiden said.

Elisha nodded. "Time is of the essence. I have much to discuss with Asa." He took a deep breath and straightened his shirt with a tug. He squared his shoulders as he looked at them.

"You don't know that transporting sigil, do you?" Aiden asked Ginny.

"No, I've never really seen it."

He rubbed his neck, pocketing the ring with a shaky hand. "Then we better get walking."

Chapter 4

Aiden's heart beat faster and his hands curled into fists as they walked into the chapter house. Where was Asa? This was all his fault. They should have gone to the Keeper's house last night to save him and the tome. His face was hot as Sarai walked into the living room. Aiden had no idea where Ezra was. Aiden pushed his troubled thoughts of the ring from his mind. He had to focus on getting the tome back.

"Where did you go so early? And who is this?" she asked, shaking her disheveled curls from her face. She had clearly just woken up as she sipped from a mug.

"This is the Secret Keeper, Elisha," Aiden said in a huff. She nodded to him. "And he's barely alive, no thanks to Asa."

"What was this?" Asa said, walking into the room with a scowl.

"We lost the Book of Rituals thanks to you!" Aiden's voice rose as his hands turned into fists. He fought to keep himself from trembling as the heat rose from his neck to his face.

Asa scoffed, waving his hand dismissively. "Thanks to me?"

Aiden glared at the man. "Yes. Now Jacob has it. I told

you we needed to get it yesterday."

"And I warned you of the danger as well, Asa. You would not listen," Elisha said, pursing his lips.

"Be calm," Asa began, splaying his hands before him with a placating smile.

"You expect us to be calm?" Aiden snapped. "All of this could have been easily prevented. This man almost died because of you. We should have gone yesterday when I asked to go."

Asa shot him a look. "But he did not die."

"We barely made it in time. If we had left when you wanted, Elisha would be dead."

"What matters is that you did make it in time."

Aiden gritted his teeth.

"Asa is right," Sarai said in a soothing voice. "Elisha is fine. " She looked from Aiden to Asa, frowning. "Asa did nothing wrong. You are overreacting." She stepped closer to Asa, placing a hand on his arm.

"But the tome is missing. And what's worse is it's in the hands of Jacob," Ginny said, clearing her throat. She gave Aiden a cautious look.

"Jacob?" Sarai raised a brow.

"He's a half-demon and powerful too. He is after the tomes and killing our Keepers," Aiden answered bitterly.

"It is imperative we get the tome back." Elisha took a step towards Asa. His voice was pleading and he held his hands out before him. "There can be no doubt about this. We must get it back from that demonspawn."

"Do you know where he would have gone?" Ginny asked.

"How are we to know this? It is an impossible task," Asa interrupted before anyone could answer.

Elisha shook his head. "Not impossible. He will go after the final tome, the Book of Infernal Rituals. It is a very dangerous book in his hands indeed."

"Do you know where it is?" Aiden asked. That was their only hope.

"I have a clue. It is revealed in the second tome." He took a breath. "The third tome lies where the angel can be called. Where the fires of the Earth grew caves of lava. In the

West, in the New World, it is found."

"I need to call Jackson," Aiden said after some thought. Jackson would know what the clue meant, he was sure of it. And he needed to know about the stolen tome. "Excuse me."

He walked into the study because it was closer and more convenient than his room. Closing the door behind him, he pulled out his phone, suddenly weary. He sat down behind the desk, littered with papers. Asa was not as organized as Jackson. One of his many faults.

"Aiden," Jackson's voice greeted him, and despite the miles between them, it still helped to soothe his temper.

"Jacob got the Book of Rituals. Asa refused to take us last night. We had to go by ourselves this morning. He said he wanted breakfast." He couldn't keep the anger from his voice. "We saved the Secret Keeper, but just barely. He was dying before Ginny put a healing sigil on him."

Jackson paused. "He refused to take you? Both last night and this morning?"

"Yeah, it was ridiculous. I told him how important it was. We had to squeeze the location out of him just to go this morning. We ran into Jacob just as he was leaving with the book." Aiden clenched his free hand into a ball.

"Are you two alright?" Concern was etched in his voice.

"Fine, but angry. Elisha, the Keeper, says he warned Asa the tome was in danger, but he didn't listen. Now Elisha thinks Jacob will be after the last one."

Jackson sighed. "Unfortunately, we have no clue where that is."

"We do," Aiden said, repeating what Elisha had told them.

"It is clear that it is referring to America. And the lava caves are a big clue as to where. It is actually right where you are going next. Bend, Oregon. Your visit to see Ginny's mother is now more important than ever. We will move your visit up as soon as we can."

They had planned on stopping there, so Ginny could see her mother before they returned home. Ginny's mom was hiding out since Jacob had tried to kidnap her to get to

Ginny. She had nearly died in the encounter before Ginny had unleashed the Spirit to kill the changelings they were fighting. The chapter head was an old friend of Jackson's and had agreed to protect Helena. Now the stop held more than just personal significance for them.

"I didn't realize it was an important enough chapter to house a tome," Aiden said.

"You will see why when you get there," was Jackson's only reply.

Aiden tapped his fingers on the pile of messy papers while he thought about that and it shifted. A few letters slipped out, one of which was marked on the bottom with a dirty, inky looking thumbprint. Aiden's blood ran cold. He pulled the letter out to make sure of what he was seeing. The letter was signed in blood that was almost black, demon blood.

"You won't believe what I just found in Asa's office," he said in a low voice. He glanced quickly to the door, getting up to listen for a minute for voices. They were coming from the living area, so he knew the others were occupied and far enough away to tell Jackson.

"What did you find?"

"A letter, listen to this.

"*A new world order, where the superior species will rule above the mundane human creatures, is upon us. If you will pledge your service to me, you will receive a powerful position when I reorder life as we know it. I need the Eternal Tomes to secure my leadership. Ensure that I get them, and I will ensure your wildest dreams will all come true. The Alliance is a thing of the past. Look to the future, your future.*

"It's signed with a black blood thumbprint. It's from Jacob, it must be. No human has blood like this."

"Secure the letter, Aiden. I am calling the Bethlehem Council."

Aiden folded the letter with a grimace and put it in his back pocket. He stared at the phone, almost unable to register what had just happened. Asa had delayed them going to the Keeper's house so Jacob could get the book. His mind raced with the implications. Asa was an important member of the Alliance, being the head of a major chapter like Bethlehem, known for its significance and influence. This betrayal was huge and would have repercussions throughout the Alliance. And if Asa could be turned, who else could be or had already? But he couldn't stay in here, it would make Asa suspicious. He made his way back to the living room, schooling his face into a mask, even as his heart raced.

"You do not know what you speak of," Sarai said in a loud voice.

Ginny rolled her eyes. "I don't understand why either of you are acting like this."

"Are you accusing us of something? You, who are not even a member of the Alliance?" Sarai shouted.

"And you are a member, yet you don't want to get the tome back? How does that even make sense?"

"We must get it back," Elisha said, gesturing wildly with his hands. "It is a sacred book that we cannot afford to lose. It is dangerous in the hands of a demon."

"Half-demon," Asa corrected. "And he already has it. You know nothing of this third tome except for a meaningless clue."

"It is not meaningless," Aiden interrupted. "Jackson knows exactly where it is."

Asa waved his hand in the air. "Jacob may already have it. He is there, and you are here."

"And how do you know this?" Aiden narrowed his eyes at Asa.

Asa scowled at him. "Do you not think he would go after the third tome? Do you think he would stay here? It was you who said he would go after the last tome."

"We can find Jacob later when he comes to find me," Ginny said, quieting the room. Everyone looked at her in shock. "What?" she looked around. "I know he's still after me, but we can use it to our advantage if we need to." She crossed her arms and jutted out her chin.

"What would you know about it?" Sarai said with a laugh. "You are not a member."

"And yet I am the daughter of Grace. Can you say the same?"

"Daughter or no, you know nothing of this." Sarai

insisted.

"And yet I know Jacob is after me. He needs me for something. We can use that."

Sarai crossed her arms and looked away.

Asa raised his brow. "And how can you control his actions? You cannot use this to your advantage."

"You seem insistent that there's nothing we can do to stop him. I wonder why?" Aiden asked. Asa didn't answer, glaring at him with his mouth open.

"There must be something we can do," Elisha said.

There is. But first we must deal with Asa.

Everyone simmered and avoided eye contact with each other. There was a loud knock on the door. Elisha and Ginny jumped.

"I'll see who it is," Sarai said, moving towards the door. "Daniel and Eli," her voice traveled back to them, registering shock. "What are you doing here?"

"We are here on business, take us to Asa," a gruff voice answered.

"They work for our police detail," Asa explained nervously, still not meeting anyone's eyes.

Two tall men with matching frowns entered. They were formidable looking with their muscles and no nonsense glares. Sarai followed them silently, eyes wide.

"You must be Aiden," the man in the red shirt said.

"We hear you have something for us." The other man looked at him expectantly, his stare intense.

Aiden pulled out the letter and handed it to him. Asa stared open-mouthed at them.

"What is that?" Asa demanded.

The man read the letter out loud into stunned silence and turned to Asa. "Why don't you tell us what this is?" He showed Asa the blackened thumb print. His face went white and his chin moved up and down as he tried to find the words he needed to get out of this situation.

"That's from Jacob," Ginny said in a hushed voice. Everyone looked on in shock. Sarai's gasp was audible.

Elisha fell into a nearby chair, cradling his head in his hands. "You were with Jacob this whole time? You knew."

"What does that mean?" Sarai's voice was high. "Asa,

what is this?" Her eyes gleamed as she searched his face.

Asa refused to meet her gaze, just clearing his throat. He tugged at the hem of his shirt repeatedly.

The man in the red shirt spoke next. "Asa, you are being taken into custody on charges of treason and conspiracy. In effect immediately, you will no longer be acting head of this chapter. Come with us."

Asa seemed like he wanted to fight them, looking wild for a moment. But he let them take either arm and lead him out of the house. He never even said a word in protest.

Sarai burst into tears, wringing her hands as she watched him shuffling away.

"This I could never believe unless I had seen it myself," Elisha mumbled, swiping his hand down his face. "And yet, it is happening now."

"It's why he refused to help you," Aiden said stonily.

"Now what happens?" Ginny asked, looking around.

"Now I must find Ezra." Sarai sniffed. She stalked off, looking livid.

Chapter 5

Grace looked into the crowd with dread.

"You'll never stop us," the redhead in front of him menaced, a snarl marring her pretty face. Then her hand lashed out and touched a tall, blond man.

"You can never stop us. Not without revealing your power," the blond said, bumping into a skinny brunette.

She turned to hiss at him. Grace reached out and touched her, dispelling the Nephilim from her, but the demon spirit simply entered another body at the edge of the crowd. Some of the Nephilim—sons of fallen angels and mortal women—were turned into demonic spirits after the flood and were now possessing body after body in this continuous crowd of innocents in order to keep Grace occupied. New York City was always crowded, and the Nephilim were using it to their advantage now. Grace had been trying to free the humans for weeks now, unable to help Ginny and the Alliance when they needed him so much. But he couldn't use his full powers in public like this. He couldn't free the entire crowd at once. And this was turning costly. The longer he was away from Ginny, the more danger she was in.

Ginny, his daughter. A flood of worry washed over him, his heart beating faster at the thought of her. That half demon was after her, and his plans had to be stopped at all costs. Still he couldn't leave these people like this. He heaved a sigh. He needed a plan to deal with the Nephilim, but had no time to think of one as the spirits attacked each other, threatening the innocents with actual harm.

He rushed to a fighting couple, laying his hands on them. The spirits were cast into the air, but dove back into the crowd. He sped over to another spat, repeating the process over again. The day fell to dusk, the passing humans oblivious to their own torment.

How many days had this trial repeated already? Grace was weary down to his bones. He had so much on his mind. How many days before he could dispel the Nephilim more permanently? He moved throughout the crowd so quickly he was a blur of color. And still the spirits danced around him, laughing and shouting derision. His heart sank.

A victim screamed and fell to the ground spasming. He rushed to her, a twenty-something blonde, and laid his hands on her. The spirit was expelled from her body and she looked up at him, confused. A couple stopped to watch.

"Take it easy, you've just had a nasty fall," he said with a smile, trying to ease her concern.

She sat up slowly, putting a hand to her head. "I'm so clumsy."

"Do you think you're okay to stand now?" He had already healed her, the color returning to her cheeks. He couldn't let any Nephilim leave the area while he was helping her. He had to keep them contained.

"Yes, thanks." She stood with his help and walked away with a small wave. He watched her go for a second, happy he could help her. Now, if only he could help them all.

Chapter 6

Johnny. The word passed through Jacob's mind like a bullet. Johnny, his middle school friend with fiery red hair and bucked teeth. His only real friend at all. Marta was his companion sure, but she never resembled anything close to caring. What a long time to spend with someone so cruel. Johnny had been kind. He'd brought Jacob cookies when they met in the stand between their houses. Told Jacob scary stories and made him laugh, the only person who could do so.

Precious. That's what he had been. So much so that Jacob had given him his own precious blood. Three times. Three times before Marta had caught them.

"Can I have some more? It makes me feel… it makes me feel so powerful." Johnny shook the curls from his eyes and laughed. The sound echoed through the trees, and Jacob smiled.

"Sure, here." Jacob pulled out a pocket knife and cut his wrist. "Just don't tell anyone."

"Never." Johnny gulped greedily and Jacob bit his lip. The cut would heal soon and stop stinging. He could deal with the pain for his friend's sake.

"That's good stuff," Johnny said with a shiver. His eyes were black holes and his cheeks were flushed red.

"You're getting stronger."

Johnny grinned. "I can feel it."

"Too strong." Marta's voice cut through the clearing. "Jacob, you know better than this." Marta gave him a dangerous look, and it froze Jacob. He couldn't move, he couldn't speak. He watched in growing horror as she approached them, her grey and black hair drawn severely back from her scowling face, mouth set in a grim line under her hooked nose.

"Your mom," Johnny hissed, wide eyed. But he didn't move either.

Jacob wished Johnny would get up and run before it was too late. But his mouth was glued shut. All he could do was watch.

Marta removed a knife of her own out of her pocket and cut her finger. She bent over and drew a sigil on the ground and Jacob's blood ran cold. Two black demons crawled out of the dirt.

"Destroy him," Marta said, pointing at Johnny.

The two demons were shaped like rabid dogs and they pounced on the boy, ripping his flesh with their rows of teeth. Johnny screamed, high pitched as only a child can. But bites alone wouldn't kill him, not with Jacob's blood fresh in his system. Marta knew this.

She let the demons have their fun for five agonizing minutes. Then she said one word and demonic fire rose, black and searing, and covered Johnny and the demons, who squealed with delight as the flames roared up and consumed Johnny. He screamed and burned away into nothing, right before Jacob's eyes. The neighbors searched for little Johnny for days. Then the snows settled in. Eventually, his family moved away and only the memory of his friend remained.

Jacob rinsed his face in ice cold water, trying to wash away the memories. He'd never had a friend again after that encounter. He couldn't afford to. Emotions were for the weak, and only the worthy could now taste his blood. Only those fit for becoming demons. It was the fate of all change-lings upon their death. *No more mistakes.*

Jacob had seen Johnny once after Marta had killed him. His father had shown Johnny in hell in Jacob's dream. He'd been misshapen, the boy he knew hunched and attached to the body of the dog demons who'd attacked him. His face was a sneer of fangs and hatred. Jacob could still remember that image to this day.

He wiped his face and hands on a towel and stalked out of the bathroom. He needed to find a sigil from the Book of Rituals. It bonded two people together and it would bring him Ginny. He had the perfect plan to get what he needed thanks to his spies in the Alliance house. He whistled as he found Marta, pouring over the book.

"Any luck?" he asked, plopping onto the couch next to her.

"I've found what you need. It is just as I remember." Marta fingered a passage. "A bonding ritual to tie one's thoughts to another. First you get one personal item of theirs, the more important the best. Then, write sigil on item." She showed him the word written in the book.

"Sounds simple enough."

"You will use the girl?"

The corner of his mouth curled up. "Yeah, nothing like love as a motivator."

"She will be easily convinced," Marta said, nose upturned.

"And once she is, Ginny will be mine." Jacob grinned from ear to ear.

Chapter 7

There was a spy at Alliance chapter house in Lockewood, and Ari returned to his room smiling, slicking his pale blond hair behind his ear. Ari was the only son of the man who had been kicked off the Council. A job that had been passed down through his family for generations. A job that he would now likely never have. Nor would he have the power and prestige that came with the title. A fact that had to be remedied, and quickly. It was past three in the morning, the perfect time for Ari to carry out his mission. It was just after everyone went to bed and just before anyone else got up to start their day. The only thing that greeted Ari was darkness and silence. That was when he crept from bedroom to bedroom, leaving letters for everybody to read. Letters to sow dissent and cast a critical eye on the joke that was the new Council. *Aiden and the new Council must be brought down. No matter what.*

They may have disbarred his father, but he was still very much in the know of everything that went on at Alliance house and on the Council. He had placed listening sigils and recording devices in unseen places to this purpose when he was still on the Council.

And he wasn't alone. His father had found a new ally who was powerful indeed, and had promised much to both Ari and his father. It was he who wrote the letters Ari distributed, clever as they were, accusing Aiden of being the spy and Jackson of aiding Aiden. It was Jackson's fault really, he had always treated Aiden unfairly and had no business being on the Council. *And Aiden has no right being in the Alliance, the dirty human.*

Ari kicked off his shoes and reread the latest letter he'd passed out copies of.

Aiden, the cur not to be trusted, has yet again failed us. He is overseas and charged with retrieving something precious to all Alliance internationally, the Book of Rituals. Not only has he failed to do so, but he also allowed our greatest enemy to get his hands on it instead. That's right. Jacob is now in possession of two invaluable treasures of the Alliance. What else will Aiden mess up next? Seems convenient both tomes are now in Jacob's possession. Almost as if that was Aiden's goal all along.

Jacob is stronger than ever and our loss is great, thanks to Aiden and those foolish enough to support him, time and time again. Stop allowing Aiden to abet Jacob, and stop allowing Jackson to hide Aiden's true nature. We need a Council that works for the Alliance. Wake up!

Ari set the letter down and pulled out his phone. He texted his father that he'd had a successful night. His father told him to await his next mission. Ari was glad to finally be doing something to actively expel Aiden from the group. It had been such a bitter defeat when his father had been unable to and had been kicked off the Council by the angel instead. Aiden wasn't even angelborn. Yet the angel had chosen him over his father? The whole notion was ridiculous.

His family had served on the Council for generations. To be treated so unceremoniously was too much to bear. Ari's hands curled into fists at the thought.

Well, they were fighting back now. Not only would his father regain his position, but Ari had been promised his own seat of power. He could hardly wait. Wait and see how that measly human would dare to treat him then. His hands relaxed and he sprawled out on his bed, his top sheet crumpled at his feet. And wait and see what Ginny thinks of him then. Surely she would see he was of better pedigree than

Aiden, a mere mortal. And didn't they deserve more than mortals? They were better than humans, stronger, purer. This system was antiquated, putting humans first. It needed an update, and Ari was pleased to be a part of that.

His father didn't approve of Ginny. Ari didn't really understand why except she always seemed to take Aiden's side. But she was blinded by the fact that Aiden had "saved her" from Jacob. What she didn't seem to realize was that Ari could have easily done the same thing. But she would see reason in the end. They all would. And Ginny, the daughter of the angel, was the only partner befitting him in his new place of power.

Chapter 8

The last couple of days after Asa had been arrested had been uncomfortable for Ginny to say the least. Sarai drifted here and there, like a spirit with watery eyes and a shaky voice. Ezra was even quieter and more brooding than usual. And Ginny and Aiden were stuck there, strangers in this house and responsible for Asa's capture. It had been the right thing to do, but now the house they stayed in felt hostile to them.

The feeling of not belonging was pervasive and well-tended in the slights Sarai would often say in front of Ginny and in how she would leave the room if Ginny tried to talk to her about anything.

Ginny couldn't wait to move onto Bend. They needed to protect the last tome, and she'd be able to see her mom, whom she missed dearly. She was very invested in leaving and had been packed and ready to go since Asa's departure. Their last night in Bethlehem found her and Aiden in the olive grove.

Many fingered trunks sprouted to hale green leaves in the grove before them. The smell of the moist, loamy soil that housed the trees was calming and Ginny felt herself starting to relax. She was still a bit on edge. She wouldn't fully relax until they had all the tomes back and were safe home.

"We should have left days ago," she muttered, spinning an olive leaf between her fingers.

"Jackson tried, but couldn't book an earlier flight," Aiden said with a shrug. He tapped his foot against the bulbous trunk of the tree in front of him.

"Too bad we can't travel like Jacob. You'd think someone would know how to."

"The Secret Keeper knew, but he's dead. Besides, it's not likely they would have taught us, now would they? We're just kids."

"We're the ones on this mission," she said with a pout. Aiden smiled at her, and the corner of her mouth turned up in reply.

"That's better. It's our last night here. Try to enjoy it."

She sighed and lounged deeper in her chair. The sun was just setting in a blaze of scarlet orange and deepening blues as a clean breeze swept through the grove. She had to admit the view was breathtaking.

Ezra walked out of the door and approached them. "If you will please come inside, we have prepared something for your last night," he said quietly.

Ginny shot Aiden a look, but got up and followed Ezra. Sarai was waiting, dressed in what Ginny guessed was a traditional dress. The gold bracelets on her wrists jangled like bells as she waved them in.

"Please join us in welcoming you to our chapter." She cleared her throat. Her hazel eyes shone as she met their gazes. "We had foreseen a very different welcome for you, but wanted to welcome you into our family nonetheless. Enter and be greeted, Evangeline and Aiden." Ginny stifled a groan at the use of her real name and lined up next to Aiden as she was directed.

Sarai carefully lit three white wax candles that stood on the dining room table. Ezra walked behind them and draped white shawls around their shoulders. Then Sarai began singing in a clear voice. Ginny didn't understand the words, but the song was beautiful. Simple yet soulful. The words rose to the heavens before ending on a sweet note.

Ezra picked up a brush from the table, dipping it into

a shallow bowl.

"Hold out your arms." He pushed the shawl out of the way and painted a sigil on Ginny's right forearm in brown ink. Then he painted another on her other arm. He repeated the process with Aiden.

"This," he said holding Ginny's right hand, "says welcome." He gestured to her left arm. "This speaks of promise, our promise with heaven to protect men from demons. Welcome to our chapter and do not forget our sacred duty."

Sarai put out the candles. "You are both now one of us in the eyes of God."

"Thank you," Ginny said, unsure of what to say.

Sarai shook her head, but held her tongue. Ginny had felt the beauty of the ceremony, but was as eager as ever to leave this house.

"I will be taking you both to the airport tomorrow morning," Ezra said in a gentle voice. *What responsibility would fall on him now? Would he be able to handle it?* Ginny worried, but smiled at him. His world had just been turned upside down. She didn't know what this meant for him, but she wished him well.

"That's an early day tomorrow," Aiden said. "We should all get our sleep."

Ginny nodded and let Aiden guide her upstairs to her room.

He paused at her door. "Do you really think we'll be able to get Redeemer home?" He furrowed his brows.

"You're allowed to bring back weapons," Ginny answered in a hushed voice. "It just has to be checked baggage."

"I'm just nervous, I guess."

She grabbed his hand and squeezed it. "Everything will be fine."

"Yeah, you're right. Get some sleep." He leaned over and kissed her cheek. She didn't breathe for a minute. He gave her a shy grin, then strolled into his room.

She closed her door behind her, cheeks warm but smiling. What a trip this had been. An even longer one lay before her. But she was glad to be moving forward. They had lost the tome, but had successfully retrieved Redeemer. Which was more important right now. Jacob could never get his hands on that sword. And they would get all the books back. She was certain of it.

Chapter 9

Aiden slept the whole flight to Oregon. Bend wasn't a large city, so it surprised Aiden that there was a chapter there, but it had its fair share of demon problems thanks to the fact it was on a certain drug superhighway and, therefore, had plenty of gang activity which encouraged demonic activity. Jacob himself had a gang there and had lived in Bend before coming to Lockewood. It was Samson, the Bend chapter head, who had warned Jackson to watch out for him.

He still felt bleary-eyed and exhausted as they deplaned. They grabbed their luggage and entered the lobby to see a mountain of a man holding up a sign with their names on it.

"Do you know who that is?" Ginny asked him in a whisper as they approached him.

"You must be Samson," he said in response. "Jackson sends his regards." He shook Samson's hand. He was tall and broad, with crew cut silver hair and a wide grin.

"That bastard better send more than that. All these favors and I haven't clapped my eyes on him in going on ten years." He guffawed, then slapped Aiden on the back. "Welcome to Bend. You must be tired. Let's get you back to the manor."

"Thanks," Ginny said as Samson grabbed her carry on.

They climbed into his SUV and Aiden adjusted the time and day on his watch, a gift from Jackson on his fifteenth birthday. Normally, he wouldn't bother with something like a watch, but he'd grown accustomed to this one. Even swinging a sword felt different with it off.

They pulled up to a cream colored Italian villa style home. It was even bigger than Alliance house, which was saying something. Large windows were filled with golden light filtering through stained glass.

"It's beautiful." Ginny gushed.

Samson chuckled and parked the car. "It's not much, but it's home."

They got out of the car and were grabbing their luggage to go into the house when a black SUV revved up to the curb and seven guys jumped out. Most of them were young. They wore all black, with yellow bandanas tied to different spots on them. One had a baseball bat he leaned against his shoulder. The rest pulled out knives. Aiden threw his luggage on the ground and grabbed his tonfa out of his suitcase. It was one of the weapons he used, resembling a wooden billy club. He rushed Ginny behind him.

"Changelings?" she asked, voice high.

"Humans," he answered, swiveling his tonfa around his hand.

"Then I can't do anything." Her eyes were wide with fear.

"Heavenfire might not hurt them."

"That's not funny. If they're more evil than good, they'll die. I can't just kill people."

"Then get in the house."

"Yes, Ginny. Get in the house. Send everyone out." Samson pulled out a huge knife. He held it in his bear-like hand, looking menacing. "These are Jacob's lackeys. His old gang." Samson spit at them.

Ginny gave Aiden one last worried look before turning and running into the house. Aiden looked back at Jacob's gang. One of them had his bandana tied to cover his lower face. He stepped forward and flipped out a white butterfly knife. Baseball bat followed a step behind.

"Jacob sends his regards," bandana said.

"You are not welcome here," Samson replied.

"We just want the girl."

A voice rang out behind Aiden. "Changelings couldn't get her," he shouted. "Jacob couldn't get her. Do you really think you bunch of lowly humans can take her from us? We are the Alliance and we are infinitely more powerful than you." He turned to see a guy his age with nut brown hair approaching them. He held two aoiveae swords, one in each hand. Aoiveae was the blessed metal most Alliance used to fight demonkind. This kid was definitely overkill with this speech and those swords. Aiden would never use swords against a human. Lowly or not. He scowled and turned back to the gang.

"You don't scare us," a lackey with his nose pierced answered, rolling up his sleeves.

Two more men stepped out of the house. They carried swords, but they were sheathed at least. Aiden gave the gang a smirk.

Everyone moved all at once, and it was chaos. Samson was battling the beast with the baseball bat, his knife taking chunks out of the wood where they met. A gang banger had each run up to the three chapter members, leaving Aiden to face three hoodlums, which was just fine by him. He swiveled his tonfa around his hand, settling into his grip, and taking a step, swung up, catching a blond on the chin. He went flying backwards, landing on his back. A brunet came in swinging, blade gleaming arcs through the sky. Aiden dipped and ducked under the blade, then hit the guy's knuckles with his tonfa. The knife fell with a clatter. Aiden brought his arm high and slashed down, knocking him out. The last one looked at Aiden warily. He picked up his fallen comrade's knife, so he held one in each hand.

When he moved, it was so fluid it took all of Aiden's concentration to twist and turn and bend around both knives. One knife went high, slicing at his neck while the other went low, curving towards his stomach. But Aiden's focus was razor sharp in this moment. He dodged both and widened his stance. The guy turned into his next attack, jabbing the knife at Aiden' chest. Aiden swung his tonfa and the knife fell from his hands. Aiden saw his chance and

darted in, hitting the guy in his solar plexus hard, knocking
the wind out of him. His guard went down and Aiden conked
him on the head. He went down easily.

But the first guy was up and about to cut him. Aiden
turned, too late. Suddenly Ginny was next to him, kicking
the blond right in the gut. He went sprawling back and
tripped over the curb.

Looking around, he saw that all the gang was on the
ground in easy work but mostly unscathed, though the boy
in front of the member with two swords had a nasty cut on
his cheek. Samson took out his phone.

"I need three men for patrol. The main house. Murder
any assholes wearing black and yellow bandanas. Don't
make me wait." He snapped his phone shut and turned to a
gang banger who had just sat up.

"Hey asshole, you have no idea who you're up against
here and next time, people will die. And I don't mean me.
Get your loser friends out of here, and I never want to see
you again. You come near this property, you will be shot with
deadly intent on sight. Now get out of here." He grabbed him
by the collar of his shirt and shoved him towards the car.
"Take your little friends with you."

The guy frantically roused his friends, and they all left
in a rush. Aiden returned his tonfa to his luggage and zipped
it up. The guitar case was still in the car. He had to be more
careful with his belongings.

"Come meet the boys," Samson said, putting a hand
on Aiden's shoulder. Ginny trailed behind him. "This is
Jared," he said, pointing to a stereotypical Californian type
with long blond hair and sparkling green eyes. Aiden nodded
at him. "And this," he gestured to a handsome Hispanic with
curling brown hair, "is his partner, Jesse." Aiden smiled, and
he returned it broadly. "And this is Emmett," he said finally,
gesturing to the tall guy with two swords. He had nut brown
eyes to match his hair, which looked at Aiden warily. Aiden
forced a smile which Emmett didn't return.

"Nice to meet you all."

"Well let's all get inside. Emmett, would you grab
Ginny's bag?"

Aiden grabbed the guitar case and his discarded bag,

and they filed suit and walked into the house.

Ginny caught up with him. "Are you okay?" she asked Aiden, searching his face.

"Yes, I'm fine. Thanks to that kick."

She nodded in relief and smiled.

"We'll have a guard here soon. You won't have to worry about those hoodlums again," Samson said in a gruff voice. "Let me show you two to your rooms."

Ginny took her bag from Emmett and followed Samson to the stairs.

"You'll be right next to each other," Samson said with a wink. Aiden flushed, following him up the stairs in now uncomfortable silence. "Get some rest before dinner," Samson said at their doors. "We eat at seven."

"Thanks," Ginny said as he went downstairs. She turned to face Aiden. "Are you sure you're alright?"

"That fight was easy. Not even one changeling."

"I'm just glad no one got hurt. Even those jerks."

"Yeah."

"That guy with the swords scared me," she said with a shiver. "I thought he was going to kill somebody."

Aiden frowned. "He did cut the guy, but I guess we got lucky."

"Get some rest. You look beat." She tucked his hair behind his ear.

"You too."

He walked into his room. The walls were painted a robin's egg blue and the color reminded him of home, though not exactly the same as home. There was a desk, a bookcase, and a dresser just like in his room at Alliance house. He slipped off his shoes and dumped his luggage in the corner, sliding the guitar case under the bed. Collapsing onto the sheets, he let out a deep breath and closed his eyes.

He woke up a couple of hours later, feeling sore. Doing a few light stretches, he walked around the room to limber up. Then he unpacked, folding his clothes and putting them away in the dresser. He decided on a quick shower before dinner. Luxuriating in the warm water, he thought about what they were doing. Keeping Redeemer safe from Jacob and trying to get the tomes. Not an easy job by any means. There was no way of knowing whether Jacob had a clue the sword was in their possession or if they would encounter him here in Bend. Aiden didn't want to dwell on these worries, but they weren't easy to just let go either. He turned the tap to cold and finished his shower.

He finished quickly and returned to his room. He opened the case to look over Redeemer, marveling in the grey luster of the blade. The hilt was covered with sigils he had never seen before. But he didn't feel comfortable with it sitting out in the open. He closed the case and slid it under his bed, pulling the comforter down to cover it.

He decided to see what Ginny was up to, but her door was open and her room was empty. He made his way downstairs.

"Welcome," Jesse said, spatula in hand. "Dinner's just about ready."

"Ginny was just telling us about Lockewood," Jared said, laughing. "Sounds on par with here, but at least you get a carnival."

"Yeah, it's sponsored by the city."

"So what do you do for fun?" Jesse asked over the sizzling sounds of cooking.

"I guess I like reading. Feels like I don't do much besides train. I'm a pretty boring guy." Aiden shrugged and looked down.

"Reading is a great hobby," Ginny chimed in. "It actually makes you a better person. More empathetic." She gave Aiden a winning smile, which he returned gratefully.

Emmett, however, frowned and turned to grab plates from the cupboard. Jesse was making stir fry, and the smell of the grilling meat and veggies woke Aiden's stomach up.

"Can we help with anything?" Ginny asked, clasping her hands together in front of her.

"Nonsense," Jesse replied. "You two are guests here.

Have a seat, Aiden."

He took the seat next to Ginny and Emmett set his plate down forcefully. Aiden sat back and glared at him, but Emmett resolutely refused to meet Aiden's gaze. *What was with this guy?*

Samson entered a few minutes later, and they all sat around the table with heaping plates in front of them. Samson prayed over the food, which they didn't do back home. They quickly fell to eating.

"Ginny, how was your trip to Bethlehem?" Emmett asked between bites.

"Eventful," she forced a smile. "But they did this beautiful welcoming ritual for us before we left. That was really nice of them." Ginny always saw the best in a bad situation, and it was one of the things he liked about her so much.

She turned to Samson, "Have you heard from my mom?"

"Ah, yes. I thought it best she didn't come tonight until we are certain Jacob's gang is long gone. We don't want him aware of where she's hiding."

Ginny's face fell. "No, of course not."

"But she will be here soon with the patrols keeping us safe. I know she looks forward to seeing you."

Ginny smiled again, and Aiden couldn't help but grin at her.

"Your mom's been here a few times," Jared said through his food. "Nice lady."

Ginny nodded. "Have you seen any of her art? She's so talented."

Emmett beamed. "She says you paint as well."

"Just for fun. I'm nowhere near as good as her."

"I'm sure you're being modest."

Ginny shook her head with a laugh. "My best friend is the real artist out of the two of us."

"I didn't know you painted, Aiden." Jesse put his fork down.

"Not me. I haven't painted since grade school, and even then it was nothing to hang on the fridge." He laughed.

Ginny winked at him. "Aiden's my second best friend.

Pat is my best friend. We grew up together. We practically did everything together for most of our lives."

Pat was the one that Jacob had kidnapped. They had defied Council orders to rescue him back when Gideon, Ari's father, was a Council leader. Aiden had been stabbed through with a demon blade, but Ginny had healed him, saving his life.

"Second best, huh?" Jesse smirked.

"Only because we haven't known each other for a long time," Ginny explained quickly, her face turning red. Aiden smiled at her, entranced by the gold flecks swimming in her eye, reflecting the light, and by her own sweet grin. Emmett cleared his throat and sat back in his chair, arms crossed.

"Well, it's good to be friends with the people in your chapter," Samson said approvingly. "We all get along swell here. Don't we boys?"

"Some better than others," Jesse said, leaning over to kiss Jared on the cheek. Jared went red instantly. Samson guffawed.

After dinner, Aiden and Ginny helped wash and dry the dishes, then retired early. They spent a couple hours sitting in between their two doors, talking before bed. When Aiden went to sleep, he was finally starting to feel full again.

Chapter 10

Ginny picked up her phone and dialed the second number she had memorized after her own.

"Gin and Tonic," Pat's familiar voice said his nickname for her on the other line. Her best friend's voice was a welcoming sound she had missed.

"It's so good to hear from you." Ginny sat back on the bed "How's the studio?" Pat had been working at her mom's art studio since it reopened to help her mom out. A fire had broken out in a nightmarish scene when Jacob had tried to nab her. Ginny still remembered that night with a shudder. Her mom had almost died, causing Ginny to summon the Spirit and kill the changelings in time to save them all.

"Everything is fine. Where are you?"

"On the west coast. It will be so nice to be able to see mom again."

"Tell her I said hi."

"I will."

There was a pause before Pat spoke again. "Ginny?"

"Yeah?" She fidgeted with a pen on the nightstand.

"I know you like Aiden, and I want you to know that's okay."

"What?" Her voice went high, and she clapped her hand over her mouth.

"I'm totally fine with it. You know, for the longest time it was just the two of us, and I thought... well you know what I thought." She could hear the embarrassment in his voice, her own cheeks warm. "But I've been spending all this time with Tali since you've gone."

"You've been spending time with who?" She interrupted.

"Tali. And I really like her. Like a lot. In the way I used to think I liked you. But I didn't, not really. I know that now, and I know I was kind of unfair to you. And I never apologized for that." He took a deep breath and sighed. "I'm really sorry for that, Ginny. Still best friends?"

"We'll always be best friends, you goof. I'm just a little surprised about the Tali thing, that's all."

"Well, we exchanged numbers the night she warded me and then we started talking. I had questions about the whole thing, and she was nice enough to answer them. Then you and Aiden left, and we both had free time with our best friends gone. It sort of just happened." He sounded a little guilty.

She laughed. "I'm happy for you."

"You are?"

"Yes, don't sound so surprised." She rolled her eyes, but grinned. "I mean, it's a bit of a shock, but only because Tali has never been friendly to me. But that doesn't mean she's not friendly, and I'm happy she's nice to you. I'm happy you found someone you like."

"I'm not really sure how she feels about me," Pat admitted. "But I'm not in a rush either. I'm just enjoying her company. We have a lot in common."

Ginny could hear the smile in his voice and beamed. She was thrilled for him.

"Maybe we could go on a double date some time," he said with a laugh.

Ginny couldn't picture it, but said, "Sure, one day." Tali hated her. Had always treated her with an attitude and was really hostile to her. Ginny had no idea why Tali acted the way she did, but she couldn't imagine ever hanging out with her on purpose. They couldn't even take a class together without Tali making some kind of snide comment or literally fighting her in training.

They caught up for a while, laughing like old times until Pat had to get ready for work. Ginny hung up, grinning from ear to ear. She had missed Pat more than she would admit to herself, and it felt so natural to be back on good, close terms again. They had a falling out when she met Aiden, but now that he realized his mistakes, she felt confident they would be as close as ever. She decided to head down to the kitchen for something to drink.

Emmett was there, fixing himself a snack.

"Hi," she said brightly, stepping behind him to fill a glass with juice.

"How are you today?"

"Good, just talked to my best friend. It was good to hear from him."

"The painter?"

"Yep."

He nodded and grinned. "And how are you liking it here so far?"

She put the juice back in the fridge and smiled. "Everyone is so nice. And it's peaceful here."

"I'm glad you think so."

She shut the door and faced him. "How long have you been a member?"

He ran a hand through his hair. "Since I was ten. My whole family are members."

"That means you saw a demon, doesn't it?" Angelborn's abilities were only activated when they came into contact with demonkind.

"Yes, I did." His voice was grave.

"Weren't you terrified?"

"I was," he admitted with a laugh. "But I was safe. My father was with me."

Ginny considered this as she took a drink. It was a strange thought. To expose a child to a demon on purpose. But she supposed it might be common practice for most Alliance members. "What did it look like?" she asked finally. She still had yet to see one.

"It looked like a deformed goat. It had horns, you see, and beady, little devilish eyes."

"Sounds awful."

His lips pursed. "My father killed it of course. But I'll always remember it."

She smiled at him and he returned it.

"Now that's not a story I share with just anybody."

She blushed. "Thanks for sharing it with me."

"Sharing what?" Aiden asked, strolling into the room.

"It's a secret. We can't tell you," Ginny answered with a laugh. But Emmett frowned, turning to put his food away in the fridge.

"Well, are you ready to go?" Aiden asked after a pause. "Samson sent me to find you."

Ginny nodded and followed him outside where Samson was waiting for them in the car. He was taking them to the lava caves where Samson had a surprise for them. The secret to the chapter here in Bend.

She watched the evergreens rush by her window as they drove down a long, straight road. The road was bordered by the same conifers that surrounded the city. They slowed as they approached the turnaround for the caves.

"Here we are," Samson said as he parked.

Ginny got out and stretched, relishing in the cool air that blew her hair off her face.

Samson smiled at them, his steely blue eyes filled with mirth. "Follow me."

They trailed behind him as he climbed down some rickety steps. Ginny couldn't help but cling to the railing as she made her way down. The lava caves opened up before them, the walls were stacked layers of brown rock covered with a sheen of water.

The darkness surprised her until they reached a lit area at the intersection of three caves. One of which was closed to the public, marked with a No Trespassing sign.

"That's where we're going," Samson leaned over to whisper conspiratorially. Aiden grinned at her, making her smile.

Samson waved at the park ranger who was watching the small crowd of tourists and locals. The ranger winked back and ushered the crowd into one of the side tunnels.

With them out of sight, the three ducked behind the sign and slipped into the cave.

The sight took Ginny's breath away. There was a hole in the top of the cave, letting in light. Someone had hung a mobile, like one hangs over a baby's crib, of prisms that sent arcs of rainbow light shooting off the walls, which were gilded. Beads of water made everything sparkle. In a corner was an altar, with depictions of the angel inlaid in mother-of-pearl. It was beautiful.

"The Secret Shrine of the Angel," Samson announced, walking up to the altar. "This shrine boasts something nowhere else in the world can. A way to summon Grace."

Ginny's breath hitched again at the thought of summoning her dad. She could finally meet him. Now it was a tangible possibility, an option that dangled before her. She had a choice, but would she? Ginny recoiled from this branch of thought. It had too many barbs.

"It's beautiful," she breathed, approaching the shrine. The depictions of the angel, her father, were delicately carved. The top held a message in the angelic tongue for how to summon Grace. His name was finally revealed and written there in gold. Ginny stared at it, getting lost in its curved lines. It shook her and she backed up into the wall, not caring that water droplets soaked her shirt. The prisms flashed around her and she couldn't breathe.

"Has anyone summoned Grace before?" Aiden asked, breaking Ginny out of her reverie.

"Yes, but that was a very, very long time ago. It's not done often, and for good reason."

"What do you mean?"

"The angel takes care of a great many important things, and he should not be pulled away from such tasks for trivial reasons."

"Trivial reasons," Ginny repeated under her breath. Reasons like just wanting to see her dad. Her stomach clenched and she looked away.

"Can you only summon him from here?" Aiden picked up some incense from the altar and sniffed it.

"No one's ever tried anywhere else. We have a special ceremony for it. I suppose it could be replicated, but you'd need our sigil." He rubbed his chin then grinned. "But this is our great secret. Only the Keepers know about it, and I'll be taking you to see him soon. He looks forward to meeting you."

Ginny nodded and took one last look at his name. She slipped out her phone, hiding it in her hand and her sleeve.

"Well, we better get going. Your mom will be joining us for dinner. Don't want to miss that." He chuckled and turned to leave. Aiden followed and in that moment, Ginny took a quick picture of her father's name before shoving her phone in her pocket and rushing after them.

Jesse and Jared were almost done with making dinner from the tempting smell of curry that greeted them as they entered the manor. Ginny heard a familiar voice in the kitchen as she took off her shoes

"Mom," she called out, taking off in a run. Samson chuckled after her.

"Darling." Helena smiled, brown eyes crinkling as she embraced her. Ginny relished the moment. "How's my little angel?"

Ginny pulled away and rolled her eyes. "I really wish you wouldn't call me that. Do you call all Alliance members angels, mom?" Her mom smirked, tucking a strand of hair behind Ginny's ear.

"Well, dinner's ready," Jared said with a smile. "I'll just go get Emmett."

Jesse started plating the food and Ginny grabbed the bread. Emmett and Jared came down the stairs laughing.

"What did you think of the caves?" Emmett asked Ginny as they were all seated.

"The shrine was gorgeous." Ginny swallowed. She didn't want to dwell on her thoughts. On the temptation of what being able to summon him could mean. "The prisms were a nice touch."

Her mother smiled at her from across the table. Would her mom want to summon Grace? She loved him and must want to see him again. Would Helena consider this a possibility?

Ginny felt uncomfortable the whole dinner, though

she did the best to enjoy mom time. After dinner found Ginny seated in the den with her mom, both hands in her mother's.

"What have you been up to?" Ginny asked, giving her mom's hands a squeeze. Helena was a workaholic. Ginny could only imagine what all this free time was doing to her.

"I've been working on my paintings mostly. Some nice landscapes of the area."

"Must be hard to be stuck here."

Her mom shook her head, caressing Ginny's cheek. "Don't you worry about me. I'm worried about you."

Ginny smiled. "I'm fine, mom. Oh, I heard from Pat. He says hi and that the studio is fine."

"Yes, I've been in touch with Stephanie. That girl is getting a raise as soon as I get back."

Ginny smiled. Stephanie worked at the studio and was great. "Oh, he told me that he likes a girl." Ginny paused to give her mom a knowing look. "Another Alliance member."

Ginny's mom raised a brow. "How do you feel about it?"

"Good." She nodded thoughtfully. "Honestly it's a relief to me. And Pat's my best friend. I just want him to be happy."

"I'm glad to hear you say that." Her mother beamed at her and rubbed her arm. "What do you have planned next?"

"We have to talk to the Secret Keeper. Jacob is after him."

"Sounds dangerous."

"I'll be with Samson and Aiden. Plus they have people watching him and no sign of Jacob. We'll probably go soon."

"You should get some sleep, it's getting late."

"We have time for a movie or something." Ginny whined, giving her mom her best puppy eyes.

"We might," Helena conceded with a sly grin.

They put in one of their favorites that they happened to have at the manor and Ginny snuggled with her mom, happy in a way she hadn't been for over a month. It was so nice just being in her presence again. She placed her head on her mom's shoulder, Helena's arm around her, and smiled. Three movies later and Ginny was sound asleep on the couch.

Ginny woke up early, a bit disappointed her mom was gone. But she wanted to slip out early before the others woke up. She needed to master her gifts, both summoning the Spirit and heavenfire. So much depended on her mastering these skills.

She slipped upstairs to change and brush her teeth, then snuck out, leaving a note under Aiden's door.

The backyard opened into a garden that looked sparse this time of year, mostly bunches of brown stalks. Beyond that were the woods that surrounded the property in a bright array of yellows, oranges, and reds. Somewhere in those woods were the guards patrolling the property, so Ginny decided to stick to the trail that wound its way through the center of the trees.

Leaves crunched under her feet as she meandered down the trail. Once the house was out of sight, she stopped. Golden light filtered down through the leaves, casting dappled shadows on the ground. She fiddled with her sensor the brothers had given her for the mission. It detected the presence of demonkind, the sigil changing color for change-lings, lesser demons, and greater demons. Aiden had told her summoning heavenfire might fry it, so she pulled it off and hung it on a nearby branch for safekeeping.

Ginny felt a little self-conscious, clearing her throat and swinging her arms in preparation. She had only summoned each power once. She had summoned the Spirit when Jacob's changelings had tried to hurt her mom. The force surging from her like an electrical current and killing the changelings. Then when Aiden had gotten stabbed when they were rescuing Pat from Jacob, heavenfire had shot from her hands. Golden flames that had burned the change-lings away. She wouldn't even know if she'd successfully summoned the Spirit unless changelings or demons were around, so she decided to focus on heavenfire instead.

Clearing her thoughts, she took a few deep breaths. She remembered how her body had felt that night. How hot and how eager she had been to do something. How desperate she had felt watching Aiden fall to his knees. She concen-trated on her stomach, where the fire had started. Squeezing her eyes shut, she waited. Nothing happened.

She tried again, shaking out her hands. And again and again, blowing the bangs out of her face as the frustration rose inside her. She groaned, making a fist. She looked up at the sky through the filter of leaves. She felt nothing like power building inside her. *Was this an impossible task?*

She looked at a tree in front of her, concentrating. She tried to imagine it was a changeling. The bark was split, covered with patches of green moss as it branched up into the sky. The big leaves marked it as a maple. Ginny took a deep breath and focused on her center, waiting to feel the fire rise up.

The woods went silent around her. The birds stopped chirping and everything stilled with anticipation. She glanced at her sensor, seeing it change from white to green. *What did that mean again? Something bad.* Her heart sped up. There was only the sound of the wind rustling through leaves, and a chill ran down her spine.

A twig snapped behind her and she spun around, her breathing growing heavy. Another crack, this time to her left and she turned again, peering through the trees. Rushing towards her was a grotesque monster from her nightmares.

It was humanoid, disfigured and hunched over as it bounded at her, all protruding ribs and grey, scaly skin. One black horn twisted from its forehead. A demon. Without thinking, she turned and fled deeper into the woods.

Her heart slammed in her chest as her sneakers slid on the loose leaf litter. She could hear the demon scrambling after her, close behind and gaining on her. She dodged a tree, nearly tripping over its roots, the stumble slowing her down. Her breath caught and she pumped her arms to run faster.

She was running out of woods and she stopped, realizing she had run the wrong way. There was an open field in front of her, not the chapter house. She whipped back around to see the demon loping towards her. She swallowed hard. It was now or never. She held her hands out in front of her, bracing herself. Forcing herself to remember Aiden dying, she felt the urgency of the demon racing towards her. Adrenaline coursed through her veins and her mind cleared. A tingling started in the base of her belly, then a flame.

Concentrating on the heat, she urged it to grow, to climb up through her body to her hands.

She flexed her hands and golden flames shot out just as the demon leapt towards her. It was engulfed in the flames right when she heard her name being called out. She laughed out loud, so full of relief it had worked. Fear still flooded her, but she could breathe now as she watched the flames grow.

"Over here," she shouted, willing the flames to surround the creature. The monster squealed in agony, twisting before the fire grew brighter, consuming the beast.

Everyone from the house burst through the trees holding swords. Aiden didn't stop until he was directly in front of her.

He put a hand on her shoulder, panting. "Are you okay?"

She pulled him into a hug. "I'm fine," she mumbled, still shaking.

"Was that heavenfire?" Jared asked in a high voice. She nodded.

"Never thought I'd see that." Samson ran a hand through his hair.

She pulled away from Aiden, still trembling. She shook her head and shivered. "I've never seen a demon before."

"You never forget it." Emmett's voice was low.

"Well, let's get inside," Samson said.

"Here." Aiden held out her sensor. She took it with a smile, seeing the sigil was white. No more demons. They made their way back to the house in silence. Everyone was lost in their own thoughts for the moment.

Ginny slumped down onto a couch in the living room while the others dispersed.

"I have to call Jackson. Will you be alright?"

She nodded, then watched him leave.

"Are you sure you're okay?" Emmett asked, walking in. He sat across from her, concern written on his face.

"It was scary, but I'm not hurt."

"It's terrifying," he agreed, and she remembered how he had faced one when he was only ten. Been touched by one even.

"It must have been hard to be that close to one when you were so young."

He shrugged. "It's common enough. Anyway, if you ever want to talk, I'm around."

"I'm fine really, but thanks."

He smiled, then left the room. Ginny hugged herself and took a deep breath. She had survived.

Chapter 11

Aiden's heart beat was finally returning to normal when he went upstairs to call Jackson. Seeing her note, then his own sensor turning green had been enough to make his heart beat right out of his chest. He'd been terrified when he'd seen Ginny's sensor hanging from that tree, heralding a lesser demon, with no sign of her in sight. The fear for her life, the relief he'd felt when she was okay, both had been overwhelming.

"Aiden," Jackson's voice in his ear was calming. Reliable as always. "How are you?"

"Ginny was attacked by a demon, but she's fine." He recalled the golden flames surrounding the creature. "She used heavenfire again." They had told Jackson about the heavenfire at the warehouse when he became a Council leader. No need to keep secrets from him, though they hadn't told him Aiden had almost died and Ginny had healed him.

"Well, that is a relief of course. It must have been Jacob's doing."

"Yeah, after the attack by his gang the day we came, I wouldn't doubt it. At least Samson says they were his men."

"Yes, it was originally Samson who warned me of Jacob, back when we incorrectly assumed he was a changeling. He formed a gang there because of its location. There is good money to be made from the gangs as well."

"Seems like a quiet place for gangs."

"Most small towns have their secrets too. But there is a chapter there for a reason. The question remains, is Jacob there now?"

"It's a possibility as long as the tome is here. We go there tomorrow to get it. I don't think he knows about Redeemer yet."

"Well, keep your eyes open. Does anyone else know about Redeemer? It is imperative it remain secret at all costs."

"No one here knows about it. Not even Samson."

"Good. The less who know, the better. Samson would understand."

They said their goodbyes and Aiden turned towards the door. He was startled to see Emmett standing in the doorway, a black look on his face.

"What are you doing?" Aiden's hand clenched into a fist at his side.

"Keeping secrets, are we?"

"Eavesdropping, are we?" His face went hot, anger bubbling in his gut.

"What are you hiding, human?" The disgust as he spoke the last word was clear.

"I may be human, but I'm Alliance. And you have no right to be in here, listening to my conversations."

"As if you could stop me. It's a travesty they even let you join. That Jackson is an idiot if you ask me."

"He's a greater man than you'll ever be, you bigot."

Emmett took a step closer. "True Alliance, you mean. I don't even know why Ginny talks to you."

Aiden scoffed. "Is that what this is about? That she talks to me?"

"Don't be childish."

"You're the one eavesdropping."

He straightened, puffing out his chest. "And I'm going to find out what you're hiding and make you regret it."

"You'll regret messing with me." Aiden's heart pounded and he felt his face flush with heat. Emmett could endanger the whole mission. He couldn't let that happen. *What was Emmett capable of?* He'd have to be extra careful now. "Now get out of my room."

Emmett glared at him, but took a step back. Aiden stalked up to the doorway and slammed the door in his face.

"Dirty human," he heard Emmett mutter before he stomped away.

Redeemer was currently being kept under his bed, but sigil or not, it wasn't safe in his room anymore. After all, he had written the sigil. Would it hold up against an angelborn? He was only a human and could only do so much with a sigil. Ginny hadn't written it since she'd had no experience with sigils at the time. *Was that a mistake?* He texted Ginny.

A minute later, she knocked on his door. He let her in quietly, peeking out into the hall before closing the door.

"What's going on?"

"Someone's snooping. Redeemer isn't safe in my room."

"Who would do such a thing?" she asked, taken aback.

"Emmett, that's who. He listened in on my conversation with Jackson."

She scoffed. "No way. He's so nice and polite. You must be mistaken."

"He is with you, not me. I'm just a lowly human to him."

She pursed her lips and gave him a look. "Aiden, he's like the nicest person here."

He went cold. "You don't believe me?"

"I didn't say that."

"You might as well have."

She held up a hand. "I don't want to fight."

"Just keep it hidden in your room and keep your eye on it."

She nodded and he retrieved the guitar case. His necklace pulling as he slid it out from under the bed.

"Don't leave it in plain sight." He handed the case to her.

"I know." She rolled her eyes. Then she stopped and looked at his chest.

She frowned. "That's Jacob's ring. Why are you

wearing it?"

His hand snatched at the ring and key now hanging in plain sight, heart pounding.

"Wait, you always wear your family ring. Not Jacob's ring." She looked at him, brow furrowed. "Why are they the same?"

His mouth opened to say something. She had figured it out. His dirty secret. Or she would in seconds. What could he say?

She looked shocked, mouth gaping. "He's your family? That's why it's the same crest? Did you know this?"

His face flushed and his mouth went dry. "Only after you found his ring at the Keeper's house in Bethlehem."

"Why didn't you tell me? How could you keep that a secret?"

"Because of the way you're looking at me right now. Do you think I'm working with him or something?"

She flinched as if he had struck her. "Don't be ridiculous. But how could you not tell me?"

"How could you say I'm wrong about Emmett snooping?"

Her voice rose. "You're just changing the subject."

He bit back a reply, disappointed in her. He had just told her Emmett was compromising their mission, and she wanted to argue with him about something he couldn't change. Something he had nothing to do with. "Look, it's not my fault Jacob has the same ring as me. Don't act like I did this on purpose."

"You kept it from me on purpose."

"And I'm telling you right now that Redeemer is in danger of being discovered."

She nodded. "Because of Emmett."

"Yes. Because of your favorite person."

"Don't be childish."

"Just hide it and keep your eye on it. Unless you want to ruin the mission."

She looked at him wide eyed, mouth parted open. He leaned over and opened the door. She stalked out of it.

He closed it quickly behind her, not quite slamming it, and threw his phone across the room. *How had things gotten so messed up so quickly?* His phone hit the trashcan next to the desk, toppling it over. Aiden swore before striding over to clean up the mess. He picked up his book to pass the time, but he was distracted, reading the same page again and again until dinner. He was silent and sullen all day, especially to Ginny.

Chapter 12

Tali woke up to find a letter on the floor inside of her door. The envelope only had her name on it. Curious, she edged towards the letter, staring at the whorls and lines of her name before picking it up.

It didn't weigh much. She broke the seal and one sheet of paper neatly folded fell out.

My dearest Tali,

You must be bored at home in Alliance house without your darling Aiden. I know what you secretly wish for and I have a way to make all your wildest dreams come true. Meet me at Ryder Park by the swings today at noon. You'll regret it forever if you don't.

Yours truly,

Your Secret Keeper

What on earth did this letter mean? How could anyone make her wildest dreams come true? Her heart raced as she thought of Aiden being with her. That was her secret wish, to be more than friends. Love blossoming out of their seven years together. Her belly warmed and her breath caught as her imagination waxed on. Aiden loving her is what she dreamed about.

But who was this person who sent the letter, and what did they want? Nothing was free and no one could be trusted in these dark times. But still, could she forgive herself if she didn't see what this was about? She'd take some weapons, it's not like she was defenseless.

She paced the room, trying to work out each angle in her mind, but she was stumped. But she really had very little to lose. If the person who sent that letter tried anything, they'd get a broken bone or three. She may as well go and figure out what was going on.

She stepped into the shower and got ready, but she was distracted, and it took her longer than usual. She got out and uncovered her long black hair, braiding it before she looked in the mirror to apply her makeup. Her dark skin was an even complexion and she didn't need foundation. Just some coral to brighten her cheeks, colorful eyeshadow to bring out her warm brown eyes. She finished and walked back to her desk. To waste time, she reread the same couple pages in her book. Finally, it was time to leave.

She stepped off the veranda and out of the gate, wanting to avoid any questions about her leaving. The days were growing brisk, and she pulled her sweater closer around her. Some of the trees already sported yellow spots. Soon the streets would be a riot of color, the only comfort she got out of the decreasing temps. She crossed the block and reached Ryder Park with a few minutes to spare. There was a bench in front of the swings and she parked herself there. It wasn't long until a dark figure started making its way towards her.

"Tali, we meet at last," the man said with a grin. He was handsome, with chiseled features and piercing grey eyes beneath his black bangs. Her heart skipped a beat. *Who was he?*

He seemed to read her mind. "I am Jacob, your humble servant."

She recoiled. Jacob was enemy number one and anything but humble. The Alliance had a dossier on him, or at least his actions, an inch thick.

"Servant?" She crossed her arms and looked up at him. "I didn't take you for that type."

"The things we do for love. A sentiment I'm willing to wager is no surprise to you, dear."

"And who do you love?"

"The girl who is causing you so many problems. Problems for everyone at the Alliance. My wants are simply the solution to your problems. I am also willing to sweeten the deal for you." He flashed her a crooked smile.

If Jacob got Ginny, it was no love lost for her. She was all ears. "Sweeten it how?"

"I offer you Aiden, exactly how you've always dreamed."

She scowled. "That's not possible."

"There is a ritual that bonds two people together. A bond that is stronger than love. The perfect compliment to each other. Just what you've always wanted, Tali."

"Does it hurt them?" She didn't want to cause Aiden any pain or discomfort.

"No pain, he won't feel a thing."

"And what do you want in return for helping me?"

"I also want to use this ritual. All I need is one possession of Ginny's. Something that has deep meaning for her.

She raised a brow, her voice skeptical. "That's it?" That didn't seem too hard to do. Especially with Ginny conveniently not around.

"Yes, the ritual requires a belonging that holds meaning for the person you want to bond with. Then you write the right sigil on that belonging, and presto, your dreams come true."

She paused, considering her options. Ginny was far from her favorite person and she'd be happy to see her go. Plus, if it meant getting Aiden to be with her, it was the only real choice she had. "So I bring you something of hers and you give me the sigil?"

"Exactly."

"I'll be back here tomorrow at the same time."

He held out his hand. "So we have a deal?"

She took it in hers and smiled. "We have the perfect solution."

"You made the right choice."

"So did you in contacting me."

He laughed and watched her get up and leave.

Chapter 13

Ginny stepped into the car, unease twisting her stomach. Yet again they were on their way to a Keeper's house when Jacob could be anywhere. They'd saved the last Keeper, just barely, but had lost the tome. What would the story be this time? And then there was Aiden, who had lied to her. She had been up late, thinking about their argument. He was right that it wasn't his fault if they were related, and it wasn't like he was working with Jacob, she knew that, but he had kept it from her purposely. And then he had tried to turn it around on her because she had said he could be mistaken about Emmett. Emmett was the one always asking how she was, if she was okay. He was the nicest one in the house, and Aiden was treating her like she was the one being unreasonable. It was too much. She blew the hair off her face.

"Jon should be expecting us. I talked to him a few days ago to tell him we were coming," Samson said, driving through town.

Ginny watched as they drove past the butte, a large hill dotted with trees. Samson made small talk the whole drive, but neither Aiden nor Ginny were very talkative. Finally, he pulled up to an older white house with paint that was beginning to peel. The houses here were much closer together than the rest of town.

"Doesn't he live in a church?" Her mind immediately went back to Bethlehem and running into Jacob. Would this be a repeat?

"It's a residence, but it has been blessed."

"Is that strong enough to keep Jacob out?" Ginny asked as they climbed out of the car.

Samson laughed. "We won't be seeing Jacob here."

Ginny just nodded and followed him and Aiden up to the house. Aiden was scowling. She didn't meet his gaze as Samson knocked on the door.

"Nothing to worry about," Samson said, knocking again. "We've had men watching the house for weeks now. No sign of Jacob or his men." They were greeted by silence. "I've got the keys here somewhere." He patted his pockets before pulling out a ring of keys.

He opened the door slowly, beckoning Aiden and Ginny to follow. Ginny's heart began racing as she stepped into the eerily quiet house. The windows were curtained shut with thick, navy drapes, so the room was dimly lit. A leather couch faced a TV and the ceiling fan in the living room turned slowly, making noise.

"Jon? You in?" Samson called out as he made his way to the stairs. The quiet settled in thick around them and Ginny could hear every creaking step they took. Aiden grabbed his tonfa as they went up the stairs, holding it ready. Her heart jumped into her throat as they reached the landing.

They could see a leg sticking out at an awkward angle, shoe askance.

"Stay here," Samson's voice was steel.

Ginny's heart skipped a beat, and she found she couldn't look away from Jon's soft brown loafer hanging crookedly from his foot. Aiden paced behind her, a dark look on his face. Jacob had beaten them again and gotten all three tomes. Even with the Keeper's house watched, he'd managed the impossible. But how?

She took a step closer to the room where he was sprawled out and that's when she saw it. The remaining mark of a sigil burned into the floor. That night at the warehouse, Ginny had watched as Jacob teleported out of the room using a sigil. She could only assume he had projected himself or some of his men into the house where they wouldn't get caught. She cursed under her breath.

Ginny looked down and saw the poor man's face, greenish-grey in the dim light from the windows, eyes wide and mouth open. She tore her eyes away and rushed to Aiden, catching him in a hug.

"You okay?" Concern colored his voice.

"I've just never seen a dead body before."

"You've seen dead changelings."

"Changelings don't count. Besides they don't really die. They become demons."

"Death is never easy, but don't let it upset you." He held her close in his arms.

Ginny couldn't help but think of the first Keeper who had died because of her. Now she had another soul on her conscience. She shivered and buried her face in Aiden's neck. His scent helped to calm her racing mind, but her stomach still felt queasy. Even mad at him, she found comfort in his arms.

"Did he get the tome?" Aiden called out to Samson who was still in the other room looking over the bookcase.

"He's got the damned thing." Samson's voice was loud and harsh. Ginny flinched. This was bad, and she could feel the rage coming off Samson. This was the Book of Infernal Rituals, a dangerous thing to be in the hands of a demon-spawn. "How did he even get in?"

"There," Ginny said, pointing to the mark on the floor. "He travels using a sigil. He probably sent his men here since the house is blessed. It would have been an ambush and completely unseen from the outside."

"All under my nose," Samson thundered.

Ginny gripped Aiden tighter and took a shaky breath. There was a lot of anger in this house right now.

"This Jacob will pay for what he has done. This doesn't end here. I am coming with you to find this asshole."

"You're coming back to Lockewood with us?" Aiden asked. Ginny peeked out to peer at Samson.

"You could use my help, couldn't you? He's got all

three tomes now, and he's got the worst one of all."

"I'm sure Jackson would be happy to see you."

"Besides, you could use my men in the fight."

Aiden nodded and Ginny stepped back from him. Samson seemed calmer now. Still, she avoided looking at the body. Aiden rubbed her arm and gave her a small smile.

Samson took one look at Ginny and deflated. "Let's get out of here. I'll have my men search the residence, but no reason to have you two here." Samson ushered them down the stairs.

The ride back was silent. When they arrived at the manor, Ginny trudged inside, all of her energy zapped. She made her way to her room, seeking solitude. She looked around her room. It was comfortable enough, but it wasn't home, and she felt that keenly now. This was a strange room in a strange place. She didn't belong here.

Perhaps she didn't belong in the Alliance at all. After all, she was tasked to keep the tomes safe from Jacob and she had failed. Miserably. And now two Secret Keepers were dead, because of her. She lay on the bed and threw her arm over her eyes, her mind spinning. *What would her father think of her failure? Did he know?*

There was a knock on the door and Ginny groaned. "Who is it?" she asked, sitting up and running her fingers through her hair.

"Tea service." Emmett's voice was too bright and too friendly. She got up slowly and opened the door with a sigh.

"You do realize we're in America, not Britain, don't you?"

"My mum is British, and tea helps make everything better."

She stepped aside to let him in.

He smiled at her, his eyes the exact color of his nut brown hair crinkling, and ducked into the room with his tray, setting it down on the desk. "Cream? Sugar?"

"Sugar please." He stirred it in and handed her the cup.

"Thanks." She took a sip and silently wished for more sugar.

"I heard you saw the Keeper." His tone was light, but

his eyes were trained on her.

"He was hard to miss."

"He also must have been incredibly hard to see." He took another sip, and she sighed. The last thing she wanted to do at the moment was relive the experience. Why was he bringing this up and studying her responses? Irritation rose inside her.

She set down her cup. "I've never seen a body before that wasn't a changeling."

"It's hard every time. It gets easier in some ways, but it never becomes easy to deal with. I saw my grandfather die. I'll never forget that day." He frowned down into his cup.

"I'm sorry."

"It was years ago, and he had been sick for a while, so we were prepared to let go. You're never a hundred percent ready though."

She took a breath. "My condolences."

He laughed. "I'm trying to cheer you up, but I don't think I'm doing a bang-up job am I?"

"I'll be fine." Ginny looked down. She could still see the Keeper's face when she closed her eyes, but that would just take time. What she really wanted was her mother. "Thanks for the tea, I'm just really exhausted now. I think I need a nap before dinner."

"Yes, of course. I'll leave you alone."

"Thanks." She mustered up a smile and walked him to the door.

"If you need anything, anything at all, let me know."

"Thanks, I will."

She closed the door, welcoming the solitude and collapsed on the bed.

Chapter 14

It was easier than it should be for Tali to sneak into princess Ginny's room. If there was any resistance, she'd have to question just what she was doing in the first place. But this was a piece of cake.

The necklace Ginny had worn up until she started training was just lying on the top of her dresser. Easy pickings. It had a sun pendant dangling from a silver chain. It was perfect for the job.

She pocketed the necklace and glanced around her. Ginny's room was far from the others. She scowled at her surroundings. It was like Ginny had contaminated everything she touched, and this room was rank with her poisoned personality already. Even though it lacked any real personal effects of Ginny's, Tali scowled at the room's mint walls and unmade bed. Tali walked out and left quickly.

She snuck out the back, making her way to the park. Her heart beat faster than normal, and she kept looking around her, palms sweaty despite the fact she could see her breath hanging in the air. No one could see her meeting Jacob.

She arrived a few minutes early and sat on the bench, tapping her foot. This time she saw him coming and straightened at his approach.

"Hello, gorgeous," he said, sitting next to her.

She scoffed. "You have the sigil?"

"You have what I want?"

"Of course." She dug her hand into her pocket and pulled out the necklace.

"Perfect," he said in a hush, taking it from her. He slipped her a piece of paper. "Just write this on his belonging. Viola."

She grabbed it and stuffed it into her pocket. "They aren't back yet, you know."

He raised a brow. "And when do you expect them back?"

"Tomorrow at five."

He nodded. "Much obliged."

She rose abruptly and walked away, the piece of paper burning a hole in her jeans. How was she supposed to wait until tomorrow? She'd already waited seven long years. Any more time was torture now that she had the sigil that would make Aiden hers. She smiled at the thought, little chills running down her spine. Her steps were light as they carried her home in no time. She sat on the veranda, looking up at the shifting clouds. Her chest felt warm with her thoughts, and she allowed herself some fantasies of what tomorrow would be like. And the day after. And the day after that. Her grin split from ear to ear.

"What are you smiling about?" Ari's caustic voice cut through her thoughts.

"Go away, Ari." She slouched in her seat, glaring at him.

"Just got a letter. It's kind of a big deal. You may want to see if you got one too."

Tali's heart lodged in her throat as her eyes dropped to his hand. The envelope and handwriting were Jacob's, exactly the same as the letter she had received from him. Had he told on her somehow? She stood in a rush and pushed past Ari to her room.

She passed the brothers, Isaac and Isaiah, with their own letters in hand. Their auburn heads bowed close to each other, they gave her a funny look. She continued past them, mouth dry. What was in those letters?

Finally, she opened her door and saw the envelope on the floor. Grabbing it with hasty fingers, she ripped it open.

Grave news. Grave news indeed. You may or may not be aware of the spy in our midst. Jacob has been apprised of every move before it happens, causing distress to say the least to the Alliance. Jackson and the rest of the so-called Council have attempted to cover this up time and time again. Why? You might ask. Because Jackson himself is at the heart of this scheme.

You'll remember who it was that made a mere human such an integral part of the Alliance despite years of vehement opposition and protest. Now we can reveal Aiden himself as the spy. Aiden, who is even related to Jacob! They are family. Jacob, like Aiden, comes from the same line of Kings, nephew to Aiden's great grandmother. This villain lies among us. He must be purged.

Tali couldn't believe her eyes. It couldn't be true. It just couldn't. She took out her phone and dialed through tears in her eyes and waited.

"Tali?" Aiden's voice filled her ear.

"Aiden, I have to ask you something. It's probably ludicrous, but just tell me it's not true."

"What are you going on about?"

"Are you and Jacob related?"

Silence hung heavy between them.

"Why are you asking me that?"

She took a shaky breath. "I just got a letter. We all did. Saying that you're the spy working with Jacob *and* that you're related to *him*." There was a heavy emphasis on the word him.

He paused for a long moment. "I'm not a spy."

"But you're related?" Her voice rose, incredulous.

"And if I was?"

"I just need to know, Aiden."

"Why? Why do you need to know? Why do you think I have any obligation to tell you anything? You don't need anything from me. I'm not the spy. Believe it or don't. I don't care."

"Aiden—"

He hung up, her stomach sunk. He hadn't denied it.

What if it was true? She shook her head. It didn't matter. He'd still be hers, all forgiven, tomorrow. She just had to make it through to that moment. And then she'd take care of this lie about him, no doubt concocted by Ari and his father. They were the only ones with something to gain from this.

She picked up her teddy bear. She didn't need to steal anything from Aiden. He gave her the bear freely for her birthday years ago. It was perfect for the ritual. She squeezed it tight and felt herself calm down.

"Tomorrow, everything will be right tomorrow," she said to convince herself.

Chapter 15

Ginny heard Aiden slam the door and stalk downstairs. He was upset, again. Just like at dinner last night when he wouldn't speak to her for more than to say one word. It had been painful for him to brush her off in front of the others, especially after seeing the Keeper dead. She didn't like this tension between them.

It was bad enough Emmett was being so nice to her when Aiden was so mad at her. But Aiden's allegations against Emmett couldn't be true, surely. After all, he was nothing if he wasn't considerate, even to the point of annoyance. Snooping seemed beyond him. There had to be some mistake. Aiden wouldn't lie, but there had to be more going on than what he knew. She watched their interactions and nothing ever happened between them. They just didn't speak. *Wouldn't she know if something was going on?*

She felt more alone than she had in a long time. More so than even when she was in Bethlehem. Aiden had been talking to her then. Being cooped up in this room wasn't helping. Her heart tugged every time she thought of Aiden, which was often. She'd been in this room a lot, to keep an eye on Redeemer, like she'd promised. But she was restless. It was time to go downstairs.

Jared and Jesse were snuggled close on the couch, watching TV while Emmett sat off to the side with a book.

"Hey guys," she said, leaning on the back of the couch.

"Hola, bonita." Jesse waved at her, dimples showing. "Welcome to the world again. You've been hiding."

"Be nice," Jared admonished. "It's nice to see you, Ginny."

"Why were you in your room so much?" Jesse asked.

"Don't pry," Jared hissed.

"It's just a question."

"You two are arguing again." Emmett put his book down with a frown. "You're making it awkward for her."

Ginny flushed. "No, no. I'm fine. Just had a lot to think about. Sorry if I was distant."

"Well, you're here now, so that's all that matters. Right, Jesse?" Jared nudged him.

"Hope it wasn't all bad stuff you had to think about."

"No, my mom said she may be able to come home soon, so that's great."

Emmett beamed at her. "That is good news."

"We'll miss her," Jesse said.

"No we won't," Jared corrected him. "We'll be in Lockewood with her, remember?"

Ginny started. "All of you are coming?"

"Jared and I are," Jesse said with a grin.

"We have experience with that monster. Jacob."

"I'm glad to hear you'll be helping," Ginny said with a genuine smile.

Emmett scowled. "Sorry I can't come this time."

"Someone has to watch the manor and be here if anything happens." Jared smiled sympathetically at him. Emmett made a face.

"You'll be lucky," Jesse said to Ginny. "You'll be with the cool kids."

"You'll find I'm the best at Alliance house," Ginny joked.

"I already know it won't be cool. You call your place a lame, old house."

"It's big though," she said with a laugh.

Jesse shook his head. "All the houses here are big."

She laughed again. "You're a snob."

"I just have good taste."

"Only in men," Jared said, surprising all of them. He didn't usually make jokes. They all laughed.

"I want some sunshine. I'm going to check out the backyard again." Ginny waved and walked out.

"Stay away from demons this time," Jesse called out behind her.

She passed by Aiden at the door. He didn't say a word to her. But the sun was sitting high in the sky and a cool breeze ruffled her hair. Samson was sitting at some big wooden patio furniture with a glass of iced tea. He waved her over.

"Hello, I imagine you're ready to go home." He took a sip of his tea.

"I just want my life to go back to normal. Don't know when that will happen though."

"I can understand that. But Jacob is a big threat. Even bigger now that he has the tomes."

"You said he's from here?"

"Well, I'm not sure anyone but him knows exactly where he's from, but he spent a good deal of time here before moving to Lockewood."

"Why was he on your radar?"

"We're used to gang activity, but Jacob was in another class. Releasing demons on innocents, torturing his victims for information or just for fun. He had a changeling named Mordecai he would use to kill off rival gang members, because how could a human defeat a changeling?"

"Ask Aiden."

"He does hold his own." Samson nodded approvingly. "Anyway, this went on for decades. Jacob and his change-lings don't age, you know."

"That sounds awful."

"And we had a heck of a time trying to help the humans. They were gang members, so they didn't trust outsiders." He stirred his tea with his straw, eyes looking into a troubled past. "A lot of people were hurt, thanks to Jacob."

"What does he want?"

"Other than you? I can't say, dear. He would kill or torture a man for the pettiest reason. It always seemed like he just liked to hurt people."

"Well, we're going to stop him."

"Yes, we will." He raised his glass to her and she smiled.

She sighed, looking back at the house. "I should start packing."

She climbed the stairs, halting at the top. Emmett was in her room, the guitar case in front of him.

"What the hell do you think you are doing?" she shouted, not caring how loud she was being.

He spun around, eyes wide and mouth agape. "Ginny, I... I—"

"What the hell are you doing in my room, touching stuff that clearly doesn't belong to you? How dare you?"

Aiden opened his door and stood beside her, glowering at Emmett.

"What do you think you are doing?" she repeated.

Pounding up the stairs indicated Jesse and Jared had come to see what the pandemonium was about.

"What's going on?" Jared asked, looking from Ginny to Emmett.

"Ask him," she pointed at Emmett who was now very red in the face.

"Emmett, what are you doing?"

"He's touching my things." Ginny felt her anger rising again.

"It's not hers. I know it belongs to that human." Emmett's eyes narrowed to slits and Ginny felt a chill run down her. Aiden was right.

"It still doesn't belong to you, now does it, jackass? So why are you touching it? You had to go into my room and touch all of my stuff to get to it." She clenched her jaw, heart pounding. He had not only invaded her privacy, but he had endangered the most important mission, maybe in the history of the Alliance. "Get away from it!" she screamed.

"What the hell is going on in here?" Samson's gruff voice bellowed from down below. Emmett froze, waiting for his arrival. Samson thundered up the stairs. "Emmett, what the hell are you doing in Ginny's room?"

"It's the human's fault," Emmett spat out. "He's keeping a secret from you, from us all. I heard it. And it's something big, and he can't be trusted—"

"You have no right." Samson shook with rage as he shouted. "Who do you think you are? Leader of the chapter? Or maybe the whole damn Alliance? You think you know best and can break any rules you want? You get out of that damn room right this minute, and you stay in yours until I say otherwise."

"But he's hiding something from you." Emmett's fists curled at his sides.

"Go," Samson thundered. Emmett scampered past them.

"We need to talk," Ginny said, turning to Samson.

He nodded. Ginny grabbed the case, and then followed Samson and Aiden down to the study.

"I'm sorry, Ginny," Samson said, slumping in his chair. "We don't condone such behavior. I'm shocked this happened."

"I told you to keep it safe." Aiden snapped at her. She stepped back, surprised.

"I've been in my room, doing just that for days. I stepped out for five minutes. Is that a crime? It's not my fault Emmett did that."

"Maybe now you'll believe me when I warn you about someone."

"What's going on, you two?"

"I told her Emmett was snooping. He eavesdropped on a very confidential call I had with Jackson, then threatened me. I told Ginny to hide the case in her room after that."

"Why wasn't I told about this?"

"I thought it was a misunderstanding." Her cheeks warmed at the admission. Aiden scoffed and stormed out of the room. She paused, turning back to Samson. "You have to understand, Samson. Aiden and I were given a mission, directly from Grace himself. A secret mission of the highest importance to the entire Alliance. I cannot stress enough how important this is and how secret. Emmett put all of that in danger in five minutes, because he hates humans."

"He will be suspended from the Alliance for five to ten years, pending behavior," Samson said after a pause. "If you or Aiden feel his punishment doesn't go far enough, I will add to it." He folded his hands.

She swallowed. "You'll have to ask Aiden. I don't know much about Alliance rules or conduct."

"That," he pointed to the case, "needs more of a safeguard than your room will provide. We will keep it in my safe and only you will know the passcode until we leave tomorrow."

"Thank you for helping us."

"Of course." He flashed her a smile, but it didn't reach his eyes.

They hid the case in the safe, and Samson went upstairs to escort Emmett out.

"You can't do this," Emmett shouted, near tears.

"I can and I have. Don't make this worse for yourself."

"How can you take his side? He's just a human. He's not real Alliance."

"He was given a mission by the angel himself. Can you say the same? Now pack your things, you are out of here. If you're not done in ten minutes, I'll add another five years to your sentence. Do I make myself clear?"

Ginny slipped into her room, unable to listen to any more. How did things come to this? What was Aiden thinking just now? She texted him about Emmett's punishment, but he never replied. She collapsed on her bed, cradling her head in her hands. The consequences of what just happened rattled her. Emmett's life was completely turned upside down. And Aiden had been so cold, blaming her for what Emmett did. How could she fix things between them? They seemed in such a terrible state as things stood.

She let out a breath and shook her head. Tears escaped the corners of her eyes and she bit her lip. What could she do? She'd almost risked the mission.

Forcing herself up, she started throwing things into her bag. *Would Redeemer be any safer at home? Or would Jacob try to grab it?* She packed in a stormy mood.

A soft knock interrupted her thoughts.

"Your mom is here for dinner." Jared's voice beckoned her.

"Coming," she answered, wiping her face. She checked her reflection in the mirror before heading down.

Helena frowned when she saw Ginny's face. "What's wrong?" she whispered as she hugged her. Ginny shook her head in response. Her mom pursed her lips, but said nothing. She held her close until Ginny felt herself calm. Then they walked to join everyone at the dining room table.

Dinner was subdued and uncomfortable. Jesse and Helena carried most of the conversation. Samson was quiet, Jared's eyes were watery, and Aiden didn't say a word. Afterwards, Ginny and her mom gratefully excused themselves and sat down in the den.

"Now, tell me what's going on. It's clear something has happened."

"Emmett got kicked out for a while. It's all my fault. Aiden said he was snooping, and I didn't believe him, because Emmett is always so nice to me. Plus I was mad at Aiden for keeping something from me. Something big. And I didn't believe him about Emmett until I caught him red-handed in my room today. I risked something so important I can't even talk about it, and now Aiden won't talk to me. I don't even know what to do." The tears came freely.

Her mom hugged her close and she took a deep breath, inhaling the familiar scent of strawberries and vanilla.

"Have you tried talking to Aiden?"

"He's been staying in his room."

She pulled back to give Ginny a look. "And you can't talk to him there? It sounds like you owe him an apology."

"I do, but I hardly know what to say to make it good enough."

"Just be honest."

"I hate him not talking to me."

Her mom rubbed her arm. "Oh, darling, just try talking to him. As for what you risked, is it safe now?"

"Yes, until we leave tomorrow at least. I wish you

were coming with us.”

She tucked Ginny’s hair behind her ear. “I’ll be following soon. They’re going to use the protection sigil on me. They would have done it sooner, but Jacob would have just sent humans after me to get to you. But now that things have calmed down a bit, they are giving me an escort and will bless the studio and the house.”

“Then I can come home too.”

“You’ll still be safer at the Alliance house. But I’ll be close by.”

Ginny frowned, but nodded.

“Besides, you need to train,” Helena said in a way that made it clear it wasn’t a suggestion.

“Don’t remind me.” Ginny dreaded the thought. She had enjoyed her training free vacation on this mission.

“Is it that bad?” Her mom smirked.

“I’m awful at it.” Ginny groaned.

“You just need practice.”

“What do I do about Aiden?”

“Tell him how you really feel. Apologize and be honest. Mean it. Then give him some time.”

“My heart is pounding just thinking of it. What if he never forgives me?”

“Then he’s very petty, and you shouldn’t want to be friends.”

“Mom, you’re not helping.”

“Talk to him tonight. Before you go to bed.” Her mom rose and kissed the top of Ginny’s head. “Talk to him right now, my dear. Just be honest, even about your fears.”

“Are you leaving?”

“Yes, you have your mission.”

They hugged for a long moment before her mom left. Ginny swallowed hard, staring at the steps she needed to climb. Everyone had gone to their rooms and the house was quiet. Finally, she screwed up her courage and faced Aiden’s door. She knocked.

He opened it a crack. “What do you want?”

“I need to talk to you. Please.”

He frowned, but opened the door and allowed her to enter.

"Aiden, you have every right to be mad at me. I should have just believed you. I had no reason not to, and I didn't think you were lying, just Emmett had so thoroughly tricked me into thinking he was a decent person. I put our mission at risk, which terrifies me beyond belief. But the thing that terrifies me most is you not talking to me. I can't even begin to tell you how sorry I am." She stopped suddenly, looking him in the eyes while hers filled with tears and awaited his judgment.

He took her hand in his. "Why didn't you believe me?"

"I didn't think you were lying, I just didn't want to think the worst of Emmett. Or anyone here really. But it was so wrong of me, and it will never happen again." Her lip quivered.

He pulled her into a hug. "I'm sorry I got so angry about it. You just didn't believe me and... I'm sorry I didn't tell you about the ring. I shouldn't have kept it from you. I was just so ashamed. It hit me out of nowhere, seeing that ring in Bethlehem and what it meant. I didn't want to believe it myself, really. There's so much I don't know about my family...."

"I get it." She squeezed him back, grateful he was talking to her again.

They drew apart and smiled shyly at each other.

"Let's leave this all behind us here in Bend," Aiden said, giving her a crooked grin that made her heart speed up.

"Agreed." She held out her hand and he shook it.

"You should get some sleep. It's been a long day."

"Yeah, it has. Sweet dreams." She walked out and closed the door softly behind her.

She changed into pajamas and reclined on her bed, able to fully relax for the first time in days.

Chapter 16

Ari stared down at the letter in front of him. It was in his handwriting, but it was not his words, though he believed in them fully. Jacob had given him a letter to copy, recruiting others to their cause. Only the really important members got letters directly from Jacob.

This letter was all about the strength of their bloodline. What were mortals compared to what they could do? What could angelborn accomplish if allowed to prosper? With the magic of the Angelic tongue and the virility that flowed through their veins, why shouldn't they be in charge? That's what these letters spoke to.

Ari picked it up and read a few lines.

Are we not warriors? Do we not fight better than a human ever could dream to? Do we not have powers unknown to mere mortals with our sigils? Humans could perform paltry imitations and party tricks if they learned the Angelic Tongue, but we wield real magic. We know better, and we are better. And it's time to take our knowledge to the next level.

Jacob was supposedly the enemy, but he was the one telling the truth. Truths Ari's family had known for a long time. Angelborn deserved real power, and now they were about to take it.

Ari sealed the letters and filled out the addresses. He soon had a stack ready to be shipped out all over the world. Then his phone rang.

"Father." He answered the phone.

"You remember the chapter in Marseille?"

"Yes, of course."

"Augustine is sympathetic to our cause, but needs a push in the right direction. I want you to go there and talk to him. Help him to see the truth and where the Alliance should be heading."

Ari nodded in the darkness. "He'll be an important ally."

"I'm glad you understand. I'm very proud of you. Of the work you've been doing. The man you've become. We will restore this family to where it belongs."

"We will be stronger than ever." Ari's face hardened and he gripped his phone.

"Soon," his father whispered, then cleared his throat. "I've booked you a flight tomorrow afternoon."

"Good, my letters will be posted by then." Ari fidgeted with the stack of envelopes on his desk.

"I know all of this seems tedious, but it will work. We just need to give it time. More people join us every day. We just turned a member from one of the oldest and most pres-tigious chapters just this week."

"That's excellent news, Father." Ari grinned, feeling some of his anxiety fall away. He'd been feeling this stress ever since Aiden got his father kicked out of the Council. It was a heavy burden to bear on his shoulders.

"Get some rest. I'm counting on you tomorrow." His father's voice was low and stern.

"I won't let you down."

He hung up, staring at the ceiling as he thought about what he would have to say and do to convince Augustine to do the right thing. He ran over conversations in his head for two hours before his eyes got dry and heavy. Time for bed.

He pulled the sheets up to his chin. Aiden was on a mission for the Alliance, but Ari's mission was the one that mattered.

Chapter 17

Perdition, with its fields of ash and barren rocks, greeted Jacob once again. He followed the red rock trail to where his father, the demon Shemiazaz, was chained in the blackest pit in hell.

"Have you seen the troops?" Shemiazaz's deep and twisted voice echoed in Jacob's head. Jacob turned and walked to the edge of the ruddy cliff and looked. Tens of thousands of demons writhed and battled each other on the dusty plain below. It was a glorious sight to see.

Soon, soon they would be Jacob's and they would do his bidding, not his father's. Jacob grinned. He would remake the earth.

"Everything is going so well," was his only reply.

"It is time to end the Alliance."

He would found a new land. He was the Usurper.

Jacob awoke with these thoughts fresh in his mind. He smiled as he climbed out of bed and got ready.

Today he would gather troops for his army here on

the mortal plane. After all, Ginny had decimated his forces, killing all those changelings at the warehouse. He had Mordecai and a few others now, but he needed more.

Ginny. How he longed for her to make his plans complete. She would make him even more powerful than the tomes would. He would be even more powerful than his father. She alone would help him rise.

When he was dressed, he made his way down to the foyer where Mordecai awaited him.

Mordecai bowed. "We are ready for you."

Jacob smiled at him and led the way down to the dungeon. Bodies were laid out across the floor, stolen from local hospitals in the dead of night. Mordecai was told to get the freshest corpses and ones that were young or strong.

Jacob picked up the Book of Words, the first Eternal Tome, and rifled through to the word of life. He had created a golem before, a creature made from rocks and clay, but he would enjoy these undead ones even more.

The first corpse was a man in his thirties who had died of an overdose. He didn't look any different than someone asleep. Only his blue-tinged lips and a waxy sort of sheen to his skin belied that he was dead at all. Jacob sliced the tip of his finger, writing the sigil on the man's forehead.

After a moment, the sigil burned black and the man's eyes opened, a milky white film over them.

"I am your master, now. You do as I bid. Now stand over there," Jacob said, pointing to the corner.

The man lurched to a sitting position, then used his hands to push himself to standing. He walked over to the corner, his movements eerie to behold, both smooth and jerky at the same time.

Jacob repeated the process again and again until a dozen golems stood in a line. These beasts wouldn't need food or drink, wouldn't need rest, and wouldn't need managing. It was the perfect solution to his problems, and he even threw his arm graciously around Mordecai's shoulders, grinning broadly.

"Aren't they beautiful?"

"Yes, sir," Mordecai mumbled, avoiding Jacob's gaze.

Chapter 18

Tali strolled into Lucky's to the sound of the bell chiming above her head. Pat was in his usual spot, which she had a hard time not associating with Ginny. She suppressed a grimace at the thought and gave Pat a half grin as she sat across from him.

"You look pretty today," Pat said, face red.

"Thanks, goof," she returned, grabbing a menu. In lieu of the normal t-shirt and jeans, Pat had donned a button-up shirt, which was staunchly buttoned all the way up. He looked awkward as he tugged at the collar. "What are you getting today?"

"I'm not that hungry."

"Then what are we doing here?" She set down the menu to look at him.

"Actually, I wanted to talk to you about something." He cleared his throat. "I even talked to Ginny about this."

Wrong thing to say. "If it had anything to do with her, then it has nothing to do with me." Tali leaned back and crossed her arms, giving Pat a look.

He squirmed. "It doesn't have to do with her." Pat's face was now very red as he stuttered. "I just wanted her to be okay with this."

Tali scowled. "You needed her permission?"

"No. That's not the point. What I really want to say is that...that I like you. A lot. As more than just friends."

Silence settled between them. Her mind whirred as she stared at him, almost unable to register his words. But a part of her brain was still working, and a little bit of horror filled her. Pat was nice and all, but he wasn't Aiden. And that just wouldn't do.

"I have to go," she said, standing abruptly. "I'm sorry." It was out of her mouth and then her feet were flying out the door and back to the house where the ritual was waiting. No more putting this off. Today was the day Aiden would be hers.

She strode into the house and nearly ran into him in the foyer. Aiden was back. He put his arms out to steady her as she found her footing.

"Aiden," she gasped. "What are you doing back already? You're not supposed to be back until five."

"We got an earlier flight," he said with a shrug.

"So, you're all back?" She half hoped Ginny got left behind with her mother.

"So, you're talking to me now?" he asked, giving her a pointed look.

She recoiled, then straightened, glaring back at him.

Jackson walked into the room. "Lunch is ready. Come on, you two."

Tali stalked out of the room and into the kitchen. He'd be singing a different tune. Just as soon as she had a chance to do the ritual.

Chapter 19

Grace leapt into the second story balcony of the abandoned building where the Nephilim had gathered and were hiding. He crept into a room, making his way towards the noises below him. How long had he been battling them? Unable to take his true form with so many bystanders around. Well, no longer. He would deal with them all this instant.

Here he could use his full powers and finally show who he was. He grew taller, his powers coursing through him like a warmth overtaking his limbs. He stretched his wings, luxuriating in the feeling after weeks of being unable to do so.

The possessed humans were gathering on the ground floor of the empty warehouse. Overly confident since Grace had been unable to dispel them so far, they laughed and jeered at each other as he watched from his vantage point upstairs. He took in a deep breath, then with a prayer, he unleashed the Spirit into the entire building. The demon spirits shrieked and were forced from their victims. With a blast of wind, he scattered them, sending them off in all directions, lost and isolated once more. They were more harmless this way. Being an angel, he didn't have free will and, therefore, couldn't kill them without orders. All he could do was scatter them to the winds and give aid where he could.

The people who had been possessed, looked around in confusion, unsure of where they were or how they had gotten there. Some of them had no recollection of the past few days or hours, depending on how long they had been possessed.

Grace returned to human form and jumped down behind the crowd. "Ladies and gentlemen, I regret to inform you that there's been a minor gas leak in the building. It's nothing fatal, but you may experience some memory loss from today to the past few days. This is completely normal. But I do have to ask you to leave as you are all trespassing. Thank you for your cooperation."

The crowd murmured their confusion but began to make their way out of the building and back to their normal lives. Grace watched them go with a smile. Now he could attend to matters nearer his heart. His daughter, Ginny.

His heart swelled at the thought of her. For so long he'd been unable to help her while he dealt with the Nephilim, only appearing to her in dreams, hoping she would find the help she needed in this realm. And now she was under threat by Jacob. He would finally be able to do something. He left the building and walked around to the back, out of sight. He rose into the sky in a flash and raced to Alliance house, high above the clouds.

Chapter 20

Ginny and Aiden stood waiting for their checked guitar case which concealed Redeemer. Aiden opened it for the security to inspect the sword. It had gotten a funny look from them, but when they explained they didn't want to just walk around with a decorative sword and put it in the guitar case from embarrassment, they'd let it through as checked luggage. They'd probably seen a lot weirder things, Ginny was sure.

Finally, it rolled around and Aiden grabbed it. Ginny wanted to hold his other hand, but had no real reason to. Maybe he would hate that. She flexed her free hand, then clenched it into a fist, pulling her luggage behind her.

They met up with Samson, Jared, and Jesse who were standing next to Jackson. He looked tired, but happy to see everyone. Samson kept clapping him on the back while Jackson smiled, cleaning his glasses on his polo shirt.

They climbed into a van Ginny had never seen before, and she settled herself into the back, next to Aiden. She was exhausted, and her neck was sore from sleeping on the plane.

"So, tell me more about your chapter's problems," Samson said to Jackson as they got on the road.

"Well, we have a spy or two. They have been trying to

upheave the Council and smear certain members...."

"You mean me," Aiden finished. "Because I'm related to Jacob."

Jackson sighed. "I found that out the day we fought the golem at the Keeper's house. It was detailed in a stack of letters regarding Jacob and his origins. However, it was inconsequential, so I kept it to the Council. But there have been letters given to each member secretly that let spill that fact. I am sorry."

Aiden shrugged. "It's okay. I only found out in Bethlehem."

"The letters paint you as the spy, but your conduct will easily prove that false."

"Of course. No one can really think you're the spy. Except maybe Gideon and his rotten offspring," Ginny said. "They're probably the real spies. They're the ones who benefit most from this lie."

"We have no proof of who the spies are. Just that they are working with Jacob and his men."

"You mean his changelings."

"He uses both men and changelings. He always has," Samson corrected her.

"At least we can do something about a changeling. They're demonic. But you can't just kill a human for being on the wrong side of things. We're supposed to protect them."

Samson clenched his jaw and looked straight ahead.

The rest of the ride was filled with Jackson and Samson catching up and Jared and Jesse being unbearably cute in the seat in front of them. Ginny and Aiden rode in comfortable silence, her leg on his knee, his hand draped over her ankle. She was so grateful their argument was over and behind them. She still couldn't easily swallow Emmett's betrayal, but he was being punished. She had to let it go. And at least he wouldn't have been able to wield the sword. Only Aiden could do that. She looked over at him and smiled.

"Penny for your thoughts." His voice was low, intimate, and it sent shivers down her spine.

"Nothing special, just feeling happy. Happy to be home I guess." She shrugged.

He raised a brow. "With all the training and school we have to make up?" he asked, giving her a sly grin.

"Well, when you put it that way." She shoved him playfully and he caught her hand and held it, locking his fingers between hers. She looked away, but smiled, acutely aware of how warm his hand was against her palm. Her mind buzzed.

"I'm just glad we're both behind in homework. It would suck if it was just me," she said, clearing her throat. "Now we can study together."

"I'd like that."

Jackson pulled up to the house and Ginny felt a pang of loss as Aiden let go of her hand. She brushed it off and climbed out of the van. She gazed upon the cream colored exterior of what she could only describe as a mansion. Besides the manor, it was the biggest house she had ever seen. It sprawled across the still green landscape it settled upon, and she knew the back of the property opened up to the vast gardens and angel fountain hidden behind the house. Already the leaves were changing, the foliage beginning to shift into the brilliance of autumn.

"You must all be exhausted." Jackson addressed everyone. "Let us get you settled and washed up, then have lunch. I will have the brothers bring in your bags."

The brothers. Ginny had missed Isaac and Isaiah, the mischievous siblings who resembled each other so much they could pass as twins. The brothers had been especially kind and welcoming to Ginny, new to the house and the Alliance. Especially when the former Council had treated her so cruelly. And when her and Aiden had gotten their mission from Grace, the brothers had given them precious gifts. The sensor that warned her of the demon in the woods, the scribe she used to heal the Keeper, and rings that allowed her and Aiden to communicate with each other regardless of distance. Truly gifts indeed, much like Isaac and Isaiah themselves.

They all piled inside, Ginny looking for a chance to speak with the brothers when she saw Tali and Aiden talking. Aiden didn't look pleased, and she turned away before she caught Tali's eye. The last thing she needed was

Tali's unexplainable wrath right now. They were all greeted by a buffet of Chinese food. The smell alone made Ginny's mouth water. She was famished and hadn't realized it until now. Bright sunlight filtered in through the windows and Ginny felt at home. She ran to get cleaned up in her room where she found Isaac dropping off her bag.

"Good trip?" He flashed her a brilliant smile, his hazel eyes flecked with blue peeking out from his auburn curls.

"It was eventful, to say the least."

He clasped her shoulder. "We missed you around here."

She smiled and wrapped him in a hug. "I missed you too."

He laughed. "I'll let you get freshened up." Waving, he walked down the stairs.

And she had missed the brothers, they always knew how to make her smile. It was something she cherished. She washed her face and changed her clothes before heading down to lunch.

Lunch was pleasant. Samson and Jackson told stories of their past adventures while they all laughed along. Ginny noticed that while Tali never said anything to Aiden, she looked at him an awful lot, always when he wasn't looking. She frowned into her noodles. After all, Pat liked Tali, and she didn't want her best friend getting hurt. That was the reason this unnerved her so much. It had to be.

They all rested after lunch. Ginny took a nap, and then started to look over her homework assignments that were waiting for her. She groaned when she saw the stack of papers on her desk. School had started in late August. Now it was almost October. She and Aiden had a lot of catching up to do. She started on some of the easier assignments, softly playing music in her room.

She was startled by loud noises and shouts, hours later. Jolting in her seat, she got up and ran downstairs. Everyone was crowded around a room in the front of the house and men were shouting. She made her way towards Aiden, wriggling to get to his side.

"Who are these people? What's going on?"

"Security detail. They're changelings. Jacob sent them

here to ambush us when we arrived. We leaked information we wouldn't get here until five."

"Where's Ari?"

"Somewhere with his parents."

"Do you think he had anything to do with this?" she asked in a hush. Tali shifted on the other side of Aiden, looking uncomfortable. Ginny decided she should drop it. This was too public for this kind of conversation.

"Ari is capable of anything at this point."

The changelings were brought in and tied to chairs. *What was going on?*

"What are they going to do to them?" Ginny asked as everyone else rushed into the crowded room.

"We need to get them talking before it's too late." Aiden gave her a pained look.

"Torture? You can't really find that acceptable?"

"You just don't get it," Tali said loudly. "You're not one of us."

Ginny backed away. But then Samson cleared his throat, which drew her attention.

"Boys, you have minutes. You will not make it out of here alive. But I can make your life hell before you get there." He pulled out a large hunting knife and stabbed downwards, plunging it into one changeling's thigh. He screamed, sweat beading on his forehead. Samson ripped the knife out and tossed it up, catching it in his other hand. He stabbed it into the other changeling's gut. He shrieked and bucked in his chair.

"This is a blessed weapon, boys. Hurts a lot more, doesn't it? Now tell me what are Jacob's plans?"

"Go to hell, old man," the first changeling said through gritted teeth.

"Let me just leave this here." Samson stuck the knife in the changeling's other thigh and left it there. The changeling writhed in his seat and Ginny's stomach clenched. This was so wrong. Why was everyone just watching this? Accepting this blindly? Torture wasn't something the Alliance should do.

"What does he have planned?" Samson roared and Ginny scuttled backwards, trying to get away from him, suddenly unable to breathe.

"You don't get it. You don't belong here." Tali's voice was acid in her ear. The look on her face when she said it, disgust. Well Ginny was disgusted. She spun around and forced her way out of the door. Running up the stairs, the tears began to fall. Had she really felt welcome here only hours ago? Now she knew she had to leave.

Her foot stopped mid-step, her heart pounding.

Jacob.

The name thrummed through her, and she gasped for air, swaying on the step.

Jacob.

It was like the beat of her heart, natural and constant. It beat through her with every breath.

Jacob.

He was such a dear thought in her head. And the thought of him pulled on her. She needed to see him, be near him. She turned and walked down the steps to the front door. The crowd was pushed into the room where the torture was going on and she side-stepped them easily, completely unnoticed. She was down the street when a changeling stepped in front of her.

She had always associated changelings with Jacob in her mind, so she stopped, facing him.

"Can you take me to Jacob?" she asked, searching his face.

"My car is right here."

Smiling with delight, Ginny followed him.

Chapter 21

Aiden watched the interrogation with his jaw clenched. Tali stood beside him, smirking ever since Ginny left. He frowned. He should go after her and make sure she was okay. She'd been pretty upset about all of this. He could understand that.

The changeling with the stomach wound was already dead. Samson squared off with the last changeling, knife still lodged in his leg. His thigh spasmed and he groaned, sweat dripping off his pale face.

"Tell me what I want you to know."

"You've already failed, you fools. We've already got what we wanted." He grinned.

"What the hell do you mean?" Samson shouted.

The changeling laughed, then grimaced, coughing up blood. His body jerked and went rigid, then he stilled with a gasp and slumped forward. The interrogation was over.

What did he mean though? Aiden turned to go look for Ginny. Tali followed him up the stairs, veering off to go to her own room. He felt bad they weren't on speaking terms, but after that phone call demanding he tell her he wasn't related to Jacob, Aiden thought it best they didn't talk. His feet carried him to Ginny's door.

He knocked and called her name. No reply. Worry

began to fill his mind and he knocked again. Then he opened the door. It was empty. He raced down to the library, but she wasn't there either. Next, he checked the veranda and the back gardens, all the way to the angel fountain in the back. She wasn't anywhere to be seen. Panic rose inside him each time he failed to find her. What if she had left? She was upset, sure. But she was also in danger if she'd left.

Aiden rushed into the house, sprinting until he found Jackson.

"I can't find Ginny," he gasped out.

"Have you checked...?"

"All the usual places. She was really upset by the interrogation. I'm worried she left."

Jackson's face fell. "We have already got what we wanted."

"I'm sorry?"

"It is what the changeling said. Maybe he meant Ginny. That they had already gotten Ginny."

"You mean that degenerate has her? We've got to help her!"

"Do you know where he would have taken her?"

"The lake house."

"Yes, but which one?"

Aiden's heart hammered in his chest and his hands were clammy. Ginny was in danger. He had to do something to help her. His stomach churned.

Then it all cleared, like his mind was filled with smoke.

"Aiden. Aiden, did you hear a word I said?" Jackson leaned forward to look at him.

Aiden shook his head. *Tali*. The thought of her floated to the forefront of his mind. He needed to talk to her, to be with her.

"Aiden, you are not listening to me."

"Sorry, Jackson. I've got to talk to Tali."

Jackson balked. "What? Now? But what about Ginny?"

Aiden shook his head. "Tali's more important."

He turned away from a perplexed Jackson and made his way to Tali's room. He still had that funny feeling in his head, like it was hard to focus on anything other than Tali.

The thought of her was clear in his mind. Nothing else was. It made him want the clarity of her.

She opened the door before he could knock and let him in.

"Tali."

"Aiden." She smiled expectantly.

"I think I'm supposed to apologize to you."

Her face fell, and the bear she was holding drooped in her arms. "What do you mean supposed to? Is that all you have to say to me?"

"What else am I supposed to say? I want us to be friends again."

"Just friends?" her voice squeaked.

"What else would we be?"

She sighed, then gave him a pointed look. "Boyfriend-girlfriend. That's how this is supposed to go. Don't you want to be with me?"

"That's why I'm here right now."

"I don't mean just in my presence."

"But I like being here. It makes sense. I'm not confused when I'm with you."

She tossed the bear on the bed and crossed her arms. "You're supposed to want to be with me." Her voice was soft, and there were tears in her eyes.

He put a hand on her shoulder. "Don't cry, Tali."

There was a knock at the door. It opened and Jackson stood in its frame.

"Aiden, are you done being ridiculous? We have to find Ginny. Do you not care?"

"What happened to Ginny?" Tali asked.

"She is missing. Nowhere on the premises. We think Jacob has got her."

"I'll go look for her if Tali goes."

Tali scoffed. "Why would I go?"

"Why is this suddenly dependent on Tali?" Jackson gave her a strange look.

"Look, he obviously doesn't want to go, but don't give me a hard time about it."

"Do not give me attitude, young lady," Jackson warned.

"I'm just saying, it's not my fault," her voice rose. Jackson regarded her a long while, then turned back to Aiden.

"Are you sure you do not want to help find Ginny? Even if Jacob has her?"

"I'll stick with Tali, thanks."

Jackson shook his head and stared at Aiden in silence. "Well, I do not have time to wait." He turned and left.

Tali. The thought calmed him and helped him focus. He sat on her bed, facing her.

"What do we do?" she asked, scratching her hand.

"I don't care." He couldn't really think about anything other than this minute. Jackson had acted strange. He wondered why.

"Well," Tali said with a sigh. "At least you're here with me."

Chapter 22

Tali woke to a knock on her door. It was early, pale light outlining her turquoise curtains. She wrapped her blanket around her shoulders and shuffled to the door. The last few days had taken their toll on her, and the rest of Alliance house was in chaos searching for Ginny. She swiped her hand over her face before opening the door.

Her father gave her a crooked grin. "I brought coffee." He squeezed his way in when she didn't open the door farther.

"I wouldn't need coffee if you didn't wake me so early."

"Oh, it's only seven-thirty. You'll survive. Here, extra cream, extra sugar."

She accepted the cup from him, inhaling the scent of freshly brewed coffee. "Thanks."

He looked around the room. "I see you sleep alone at least."

"And what's that supposed to mean?"

Her father gave her a look. "Well, Aiden has been glued to your side. Didn't know if that was a twenty-four hour malady."

She glared at him. "Don't play games with me, Dad."

"I'm not the one playing games. Why are you allowing

him to behave the way he is?"

"When have I ever hated Aiden's presence?"

"This is different though, isn't it?"

"Is it that strange that he wants to spend time with me?" She slammed her cup down on her desk, coffee sloshing onto her hand. She wiped it angrily on her pajama pants.

Her dad took a breath. "You know he isn't acting normal."

"Are you so sure of that?"

"Calm down. Come sit here with me." He sat on her bed and patted the space beside him.

"Everyone is acting like this is my fault." She sat with a huff.

"Is it?"

She couldn't bring herself to answer that question. What would her father think of what she had done? He could hardly approve. Did she even approve of what she was doing? Her heart was thorny, painful. Things were too complicated, and she didn't know how to fix it.

He put a hand on her shoulder. "Talk to me, darling."

"It's all so mixed up."

"What is?"

"Everyone treats me as if I've done some horrible thing because Aiden wants to be with me. Like it's my fault Ginny's gone." She faltered. She did have a hand in that, after all.

"Does he really want to be with you? Like that?"

"I don't know, Dad. I thought he would one day."

"Is that what you want?"

"Do you really have to ask?"

He sighed. "But this isn't Aiden. He's not himself, Tali. You can't hold on to him like this."

She looked down at her hands. "What am I supposed to do?"

"Let him go."

The finality of that statement floored her. Let go of Aiden, the one thing she'd held onto for the last seven years with every fiber of her being. *Could she just stop?* It didn't seem possible. It had always been the two of them against the world. He was a part of her. An essential part.

"You can't keep letting him follow you around the way he is. It's not natural, and you've let your classes slip and your training. You have to help him find himself again. I know you can help him."

"Dad, it's not that easy."

"You're strong enough to do the things that aren't easy. You're the strongest woman I know. And I know you'll make things right again. I believe in you, Tali." He fingered her braids. "I love you."

"I love you too, Dad."

"Just think about what I've said, okay? I know you can fix this." He kissed her forehead. "Drink your coffee before it gets cold." And with that he left.

Tali got up to get her cup and took a long drink. Everyone was talking about Aiden and how he wasn't himself, how unnatural it was that he was glued to her, and how pathetic it was that she allowed all this to go on. It made her furious. She and Aiden had been close for seven years. What was so unnatural about them hanging out? People gossiped too much. But now her father had felt the need to talk to her about it. Not with harsh words or threats, but in his calm, collected way. He wanted her to let go. But she didn't know if that was even possible. Aiden was her life even more than the Alliance was her life. If she had to choose between the two, she'd pick Aiden every time. So how could she let him go now? Now when he was finally with her? Sure he was absent minded and often quiet. But he wanted to be with only her, and that meant the world to Tali.

She couldn't do anything yet. Maybe Aiden would come round and really like her. She couldn't give up now when she was so close.

Still her father's words echoed in her head. She couldn't ignore them, but she'd give Aiden more time. If things got worse, then she'd let him go.

Chapter 23

Jacob strolled down the hall to Mordecai's room. The lazy oaf was still sleeping. He slammed the door open, startling Mordecai so much that he fell out of bed, still wrapped in his sheets. He yelped in pain as he hit the floor.

"Good morning, my friend," Jacob said brightly, ready to pick Mordecai up by the scruff of his neck.

He sat up and rubbed his elbow. "Good morning, master." He struggled with the sheets for a moment before succeeding in freeing himself. "What's on the agenda for today, master?" he said, standing.

"Our lovely guest is here. You will entertain her while I work."

"I'm not very good at entertaining ladies."

"You don't have to be good at it. You just have to do it. We need to know what she knows."

"Yes, master."

"Then get dressed. And give her back her necklace. A gift from me." Jacob placed the necklace he had gotten from Tali on Mordecai's dresser.

Jacob left the room without bothering to shut the door. It gave him a small pleasure knowing Mordecai would have to. He whistled as he walked down the hall to where Marta was sitting, going over the Tomes.

"Learning a lot, dear mother of mine?"

This hawk of a woman smiled indulgently at him. "I am not your mother."

This was true, his mother had died moments after giving birth to him, and Marta had raised him and stayed cruelly by his side for the last century. Marta was originally an angelborn from eastern Europe who had willingly dedicated herself to his father long before he was born.

"The only one who counts," he said, flopping down next to her on the couch.

She reached forward to pet his hair. A rare sign of affection.

"Are you learning anything useful?"

"Much, and there is much still to learn. These books have great value for us."

"I value how the Alliance must be scrambling without them and without their Secret Keepers. Without the Keepers, they have no knowledge of the books. We have dealt them a large blow."

Marta laughed. "It feels good, no?"

Jacob smiled. "Very good."

"I have found permanent bonding spell. Your blood mingles, your souls combine. Until death you will be together. If she tries to get away from you even, she will die."

"But won't her blood poison me?"

"Yes, it would in normal case, which is why I keep looking. There is sigil to use against the poisoning. Against angelic and against demonic. Use these sigils first and both will be fine."

"You're a genius," he crowed. His plans were all coming to fruition. Soon, he would be in charge of everything he could imagine. A new world order just as his letters stated. And with Ginny at his side, doing his bidding as well. His heart lifted, grin split from ear to ear. Finally he would have everything he wanted. It wouldn't be long before all his dreams came true.

Chapter 24

Aiden had been following Tali around for days now. Most of the time he was completely absent minded, like his brain wasn't functioning. He certainly wasn't amorous. Why the hell hadn't the ritual worked? She'd copied the sigil carefully and used his bear. The thought occurred to her that it was really her bear, not his. She had botched up the whole thing.

Aiden wasn't what she had dreamed of, and everyone in the house was talking about them and how wrong the situation was. She didn't think it was unnatural for him to want to be with her, but still there was no denying he wasn't his normal self. She put her head in her hands, close to tears.

"What are you doing, Tali?"

"What does it look like I'm doing?"

"I don't know. Just thought I'd ask. I can't think of anything else to say." He shrugged, and she let out a sigh.

"You mean you can only think about me?"

"You're the only clear thought in my head. When I'm not here, I feel lost and confused and keep thinking about you. It's simpler just to stay here with you."

And now the tears did come. He didn't want to be with her, he was compelled to be with her. This ritual was awful, and a sob escaped her. She had to do something to fix this.

She grabbed the teddy bear and turned to face Aiden. "Follow me," she said in a whisper.

They made their way down to the library, which was thankfully empty. She unhooked the grate cover to the fire. The blaze inside burned brightly and she gave it a small, sad smile.

"I'm sorry, Aiden," she said, then tossed the bear into the flames.

It burned quickly, wispy tendrils of grey smoke climbing into the air. She turned to face Aiden, waiting for the change in him to happen.

He looked at her confused, as if wondering what he was doing here or maybe trying to figure out the last few days. She swallowed hard.

"Tali." His voice was a warning. "What happened?"

"It was a ritual, but it didn't work right," she began, but lost her voice.

"What did you do to me?"

"I just wanted you to like me."

"Like you?" His voice went high.

She huffed. "Aiden, it's what I've always wanted."

"Why couldn't I think straight? You did that to me? Made me into some sort of zombie?"

"The ritual didn't work. You weren't supposed to be like that."

"No, I was supposed to be forced to be in love with you."

She had no words.

"What ritual did you use?"

"A bonding ritual. It bonds two people together."

He raised his hands, fists clenching. "You manipulated me. What right did you have to try and force my feelings?"

"Aiden, I'm sorry. That's why I stopped."

"You shouldn't have done it in the first place," he shouted. Tali flinched, face flushed. "You had no right to do that to me."

"I'm—"

"Oh God, Ginny! You've kept me from finding her for days now. How could you? She's in danger, and you let me do nothing."

Tali cringed and bit her lip.

"Never talk to me again." His voice was steel. "You mean nothing to me now, Tali. Less than nothing." He turned and stalked out of the library.

Tali's heart was in a pile at her feet, and she felt sick to her stomach. How had things gone so wrong? The tears fell freely.

Chapter 25

Aiden fled to his room, mind panicking about Ginny until he felt sick and slightly dizzy. His heart thumped in his chest and he flopped onto his bed, mind racing. He had to find Ginny somehow and get her back to safety. But how?

Absentmindedly, he fidgeted with the ring on his finger.

"Ginny," her name was a whisper in his thoughts.

"Aiden," he heard clearly in his ear and almost fell off the bed. The rings the brothers gave them before they left on their mission let them communicate, of course. All you had to do was turn the black stone and speak. The other would hear automatically and could respond. He sat up eager.

"Ginny, are you alright? Are you okay?"

"I'm fine. I've never been happier." Her voice was light and breathy.

He took his own deep breath. "Where are you?"

"At the lake house. I love Lake Locke. It's so calming."

His breath quickened. "Which house on the lake?"

"It's big. And black. He's a bit morbid, you know."

"Who is?"

She giggled. "Jacob, silly. He does like to be dramatic. But I love it. I love him."

Aiden bit back a reply. "I'm happy you're okay."

"Yeah, but I have to go. He'll be here soon and—"

"You can't tell him we talked. Ginny, do you understand me? Do not tell him we talked at all," he rushed to say.

"Okay, I won't. I don't want him to get mad at me anyway. I hate when he gets sullen."

"I'll see you soon, Ginny. I promise."

"Bye, bye, Aiden."

Aiden twisted the ring, panting. He could hardly believe his luck. He had completely forgotten about what the rings could do. Slapping on his weapons belt, he grabbed Redeemer. It was finally time to use it. He just needed to come up with a plan to get her back. Jackson was much better at strategy, and he left his room in search of him. He found him outside the library.

"I know where she is," he shouted, racing towards him.

He gave Aiden a look. "Who? Tali?"

"No, Ginny."

"Aiden, is that really you?" Concern etched his features, and he put a hand on Aiden's shoulder. "Come inside, we must talk."

They rushed into the now empty library.

"Yes, Tali used a bonding ritual on me. I couldn't think straight."

"She needs to be taught a lesson. That is nothing to play around with. Another human's free will."

"You're telling me. It was awful."

Jackson rubbed his forehead. "I suppose she is one of our spies. She certainly did not learn that ritual from me, and there is no one else who would have taught her that in the Alliance."

"I wouldn't be surprised what she is capable of any more. But more importantly, I know where Ginny is. At Jacob's lake house on Lake Locke. Big black house. We have to hurry."

"Are you certain? How do you know?"

"We have a way of communicating with each other that the brothers made us. I had completely forgotten about it, but used it just now to speak to her."

Jackson gave him a look like he shouldn't keep

secrets, but merely said, "We will get her back. Wait here."

Aiden's fingers danced against his leg as he waited. He glanced at the fireplace, still fuming from his encounter here with Tali just moments ago. A deep sense of betrayal opened him up like a pit, and anger eagerly filled it. Rage bubbled in his belly and he felt the heat of it in his chest. The only thing keeping his rage at bay was the concern he felt for Ginny. That she was in the hands of that monster, Jacob, was almost too much to bear.

A blinding flash and burst of heat filled the room and Aiden dropped to his knees, hands shielding his eyes. The angel stood before him, once again clad as a warrior. Aiden's heart skipped a beat.

The angel was tall, looming up before Aiden, his strawberry blond hair gleaming both red and gold in the light. His iridescent wings flexed at his sides as he regarded Aiden with golden eyes.

"Rise, Aiden. It heartens me to see you with that sword."

"Are you here to rescue Ginny, too?"

Grace nodded. "And here is Jackson with the others."

Jackson strode in with Samson in tow and stopped, clutching his chest. "Oh Gracious One," he bowed, face turning red.

"Can this be?" Samson asked in a hush.

"The angel," Jackson hissed, giving him a sidelong glance and a nudge. Samson placed his hand over his heart and bowed his head.

"I am pleased to meet you, but there is no time for formalities."

"Yes, everyone is assembling at the cars now. Shall we join them?" Jackson asked.

Samson and his men,and Jackson and his, filed out and piled into the SUVs. The angel had changed into human form minus the gladiator outfit. He sat next to Aiden in normal clothes, and Aiden's mind spun, trying to find some-thing to say. No one spoke, awed by the presence of the angel. He hadn't been seen at the Alliance in decades, and no one knew how to act around him.

Jackson drove, much more aggressively than his usual

calm behavior. He sped around cars, weaving through lanes to reach Lake Locke as fast as possible. The skies were deepening and filled Aiden with a sense of foreboding.

"We'll get Ginny back," Aiden said in a soft but resolute voice.

Grace cringed. "He's had her for days...."

"I think he's using a bonding ritual to keep her there. She said she was happy to be there."

"Said?"

"We have these rings where we can talk regardless of distance. I'd forgotten about them, but I used it to talk to her just now. That's how I know where she is."

He nodded. "I'm glad you talked to her."

"At least she's safe," Aiden said and Grace grimaced. "This must be hard for you. It's driving me crazy; I can't even imagine how you must feel."

"Yes, this is difficult. I feel so much worry and even anger. But all that is meant to pass will pass." He placed a hand on Aiden's knee and the tumult of emotions he was feeling settled. A deeper peace swam in his stomach, and Aiden found he could focus now.

"What's the plan?"

"The main concern is that she must be separated from Jacob, for her safety. And Jacob must be stopped. His plans must not come to bear."

They neared the lake and Aiden saw the sprawling black lake house that must belong to Jacob pull into view.

"There," he said, pointing. Jackson nodded and parked the car.

Chapter 26

Tali sat in the back of the SUV with her father and the brothers. She hadn't spoken a word since Aiden had stormed away from her, and her dad kept giving her furtive looks she summarily ignored. Her chest ached, as though a hole had formed there when her heart had fallen to her feet. And she knew she looked like she had been crying, her eyes were swollen and her face was red. Aiden said she was nothing to him and it more than stung. But besides heartbroken, she was also angry, cheeks flushed and hands gripped into fists on her knee. None of this was fair. If only the sigil had really worked. Then she wouldn't have all these problems. Still what she had managed to do to Aiden had been wrong.

Worst of all, she had helped Jacob, a demonspawn. She could hardly believe her own actions. She hadn't meant to give Jacob information, like when Aiden and Ginny were supposed to arrive, which led to a direct attack on the house and Ginny being taken. Luckily no one was really hurt, but still. She had caused that. And even though she hadn't meant to do that, she had meant to give Jacob what he needed to control Ginny, and that was awful too. She knew that now and felt the full shame of her actions. She would fix this. She had to. She took a deep breath, but it turned into a sob she had to choke back.

"Are you okay?" her dad's voice was low and sweet.

"I did what we talked about." She sniffled. "It didn't go very well."

"Give him time. It only just happened."

The car pulled forward, following the SUV Jackson drove that held the angel and Aiden. Another SUV followed them, holding Samson and his boys plus a security detail. *What would the angel think of her? What would he do?*

Tali sighed and turned to face her dad. "I don't think he'll ever forgive me. Not this time."

"You should be at home."

"No," she said loudly, causing Isaiah to glance over for a minute. She waited for him to turn back to his brother before continuing. "I want to help. I need to." She swallowed hard.

Lionel nodded. "I'll be right by you the whole time."

"Thanks, Dad." She leaned her head against his shoulder as he wrapped his arm around her. As always, he was her rock, always in her corner. She didn't know if Aiden would ever forgive her, but she was glad to know her father did. She hoped she had made him proud by destroying the bear. It hadn't been easy. But she had done that for her dad as much as she had done it for Aiden.

They arrived and a restless energy filled her. They disembarked, and Tali swung her arms out while the others adjusted their weapon's belts and looked around.

It was quiet. Most families had left their properties after the summer season ended. Back lawns ran towards the beach where the grass ended in clumps and the sand began. The lake itself was tranquil, not a ripple stirring. The water looked black in the darkening night.

Chapter 27

Ginny was alone in her room, which she abhorred. All she really wanted was to be near Jacob. When he talked to her, her heart and head soared and she was on cloud nine, rising against the fog that filled her when he wasn't there. Getting any of his attention was a treat.

Aiden. She had talked to Aiden today. The thought tugged at her heart, making it speed up for a brief moment. But then the thought was pushed out of her mind. Jacob would be coming soon. That's all that mattered.

She jumped up with a smile when she heard the sounds of his steps coming towards her, now as familiar to her as her own.

"Hello, my angel," he said as he entered the room with a leering smile. She rushed towards him and embraced him. "Tonight is a special night."

"Special?" She smiled at him as he caressed her cheek.

"Very special. You get to meet my father and my brothers in arms. You and I will be united until death. And your blood will protect me."

"I don't understand."

"Your kind is afraid of blood magic. They see it as evil, but tonight I will use it to protect myself from those awful aoiveae blades and blessed ground. I will use your blood to shield me."

"How is that possible?"

"Through study of the darker arts. I have spent many decades searching for a solution to my problems. Mainly, the Alliance's ability to stop me. You are finally an angel-born strong enough to charm my demon blood. That's why I marked you. You are the answer to my problems, my sweet."

At the fair this summer he had placed a demon mark on her that had made her angelic powers stronger as her blood struggled against the poison, though it made her seriously ill. The pain had been constant, a welt on her knee spiraling out into poisonous lines snaking through her. But it had all been for a reason. She smiled at him.

"I'm glad I can help you." She leaned into him.

He pulled out a syringe and bade her sit. "This," he said, inserting the needle into her arm, "will make me invincible to Alliance weapons."

She sucked in air as he drew the plunger back. She watched her blood fill the needle, a bright red. Would he need a lot? How did this all work? She had a dizzy feeling, like vertigo. *Jacob would be impervious to Alliance weapons.* Did she want that?

But then the haze descended again, and all she wanted was Jacob. Whatever he wanted was just fine with her.

"Tell me about your dad," she said as he pulled out the needle.

"He wants freedom, and I was made to grant him that." His voice was bitter as he continued. "They're called the burned ones, my father and my brethren. Heavenfire burned my father and created our kind, demons."

"And they're coming here?"

"I need an army."

A flash of teeming, disfigured shapes battling on a dusty field filled her mind, and she shuddered at the memory. Then it was gone. "Won't people see your army here?"

"Not here. I used a sigil around the lake so that mere humans couldn't see anything supernatural occurring.

They are not special, after all. Why should they see us?" He laughed and she joined in. "No one knows what this place really is."

She saw an image from a dream. She saw the angels rising up from the water, not a ripple on its surface. And then it was gone.

He took several vials of her blood and left her alone in the room again. She paced and fidgeted with her hair until Marta came in.

Marta grimaced at Ginny's smile. She was a middle-aged woman with black and silver hair, pulled back harshly from her face. She had a nose like a hawk's beak and seemed to hate Ginny from the moment she saw her.

"We must get you ready for master," she said, putting down a makeup bag, brush, and a knife. "Sit."

Ginny did as she was told and Marta stood behind her, brushing her hair.

"Tonight important. You will be joined with the master for eternity."

"I'd like that," Ginny cooed, closing her eyes.

Marta braided her hair into an elegant knot. Then she approached her with the makeup bag. She began applying it, and Ginny wondered how the harsh woman before her even knew how to. She didn't seem like the type to have ever worn it at all.

Marta sang while she worked, a mysterious song in a foreign tongue that made Ginny drowsy as she listened. A heaviness cloaked her body and made her feel paralyzed.

"Your soul must be prepared for the bonding. Made willing and weaker," Marta said, sweeping eye shadow over Ginny's lids. "Never before has your kind been forged with demonborn." She added mascara, then picked up the knife, cutting her finger. "You need special sigil, so demon blood will not poison you or change you. It supposed to work." She shrugged, drawing a mark on Ginny's ankle. Ginny winced as the sigil drawn in changeling blood burned into her skin. Marta yanked her up and pulled her over to the closet.

"Put on this." She held out a buttery gold dress covered with lace. Ginny changed quickly and Marta buttoned up the back of the dress.

Marta held up a mirror before Ginny and Ginny breathed in. Her brown eyes shone almost gold, highlighted by a shimmery purple shade on her lids. Her cheeks were a soft rose and her mouth a full red pout. Long black lashes completed the elegant look. She felt beautiful and couldn't wait for Jacob to see her like this.

"Now, you are ready for master."

She followed Marta down the stairs and out the door to the shore of the lake where Jacob waited. Jacob was dressed smartly in a vest and suit pants. His button down shirt was rolled up at the sleeves to his elbows. His black hair was perfectly gelled, and Ginny felt a rush of joy to see Jacob standing there, smiling at her. Mordecai stood at attention at the back door of the house where they passed. Jacob held out a hand to her. She joined him, beaming.

"First, we must invite Father over."

She blinked at him, not really understanding.

He took out his ceremonial dagger and sliced a cut into his palm. Making a fist, he dripped blood from his hand. He held it above the water. It sank in black swirls beneath the surface.

"I summon you, Shemiazaz, first of the Burned Ones and greatest of your name. Cross and enter this realm," Jacob's voice called out into the deepening twilight.

Ginny felt a shiver course through her as she watched a dark shape rising to the surface as if drawn to the blood. He shot out of the still waters, wrapped in thick, black chains, a hungry look on his pale, grey face as he took in Ginny at his son's side. Grey scales crawled down his neck and back, and he had large, leathery, black wings, like a bat. Even hunched over, Ginny knew he would loom over her at his full height.

"Welcome, Father," Jacob said with a stiff bow. "We must do the bonding ritual, then I will call my brothers forth."

"You should call them now," was his father's reply in a deep, raspy voice.

"I will not wait," Jacob hissed, pulling Ginny to his side. "I need her, and I want this bond permanent."

"Then give me what I need." The demon held out a

taloned, black tipped hand. Jacob handed him his dagger and Marta gave him a black ribbon. "Hold out your hand," Shemiazaz intoned. Ginny hesitated, not wanting to. But in the end, she obeyed when Jacob nodded, hand shaking.

Shemiazaz made a cut in her palm, and she let out a cry. "Hold hands." Shemiazaz held up the ribbon as Jacob grabbed her cut hand in his, their palms met, slick with blood. She shivered again as the demon tied their joined hands with the ribbon.

"As your blood mingles, so shall your souls, becoming one in the eyes of the Most High and all. With this final sigil, you will be bound in life, in death, eternal."

He cut his finger and began to draw a sigil on her wrist. But a strange feeling overtook Ginny, like a tugging at her core. She was yanked from Jacob's side, hand sliding under the ribbon, and flying away from Jacob and his father to the side of the beach.

"You will not touch my daughter," a voice boomed in the darkness.

Ginny looked up from where she had landed on the beach and saw Aaron, her friend from her favorite diner, standing with the Alliance at the edge of the sand. Her friend who had always comforted her, had even spent a few father's days with her so she wouldn't feel so alone when she thought her father was long dead. Standing there with the Alliance, he was glowing, in full angel form, with a fierce countenance. Iridescent wings flexing in the breeze.

Father. The thought coursed through her with a shock. Her father had been there for her all along, buying her milkshakes and spending time with her. Her heart pounded.

"She's mine," Jacob shouted and Ginny's mind blanked once again. She had to get back to him. She rose and ran towards him, tripping on the sand in her hurry. "She is bound to me." She fell at his feet. Jacob grabbed her by the arm and yanked her to her feet. "If you want her back, you must give me Usurper, the sword of my name."

"Let go of her," Aiden yelled, and Ginny's heart skipped a beat.

Jacob's grip tightened. "Give me what I want." *What did he want exactly?* She struggled to remember.

"You cannot defeat all of us," Aiden answered, gesturing to the Alliance members behind him.

"Try me," Jacob said, then snapped his fingers. Mordecai fumbled at the back door, then opened it. A dozen walking corpses shuffled out right in front of the waiting Alliance members who had not reached the beach yet. Ginny cringed. They all had the mark of the golem on their foreheads.

The Alliance members engaged them, hacking away with gleaming aoiveae swords. Ginny held her breath.

Aiden lobbed off the arm of one golem as it reached out to strangle him. Jackson beheaded another with one clean strike. It toppled to the ground. Isaac grappled with a dead woman. The corpse bucked and writhed under his grip. Jesse stabbed a corpse straight through its heart, having no effect. It threw a punch and sent him back reeling, his sword still stuck through it.

Tali broke free from the pack and raced towards them.

"Glad you're seeing sense and joining the winning side," Jacob said with a smile. Tali grimaced, then ripped the necklace from Ginny's throat.

The fog lifted and Ginny watched in horror as Jacob pulled out the sword at his side and stabbed Tali through her stomach. Tali gasped as Jacob pulled the sword out, dripping red, and she crumpled to the ground.

"Tali!" Aiden cried, slashing a golem to pieces and breaking free from the fight. He held Redeemer in his hand as he ran towards them. Lionel was battling three at once.

"The sword," Shemiazaz growled behind Ginny.

"Give me the sword and you can help your friend." Jacob said as Aiden met them.

"Don't do it, Aiden. I don't deserve to live. This is all my fault," Tali gasped in tears.

"Don't be ridiculous." Aiden's voice was choked.

"It's almost over," Jacob said with a maniacal grin.

Ginny wiped tears from her eyes as Tali sputtered, a large pool of blood surrounding her. Her hand automatically went for her scribe, but Jacob had taken that from her the day she had arrived. And she had no knife of her own to heal Tali with her blood.

"You can't wield it." Aiden looked at Jacob determined.

"All you have to do is free my father."

Aiden paused for just a moment, his face twisted, as if in pain, then he stepped forward and swung. Ginny turned to see the demon holding out his chain. Her heart raced. The one thing they didn't want to happen was about to come true, and there was nothing she could do to stop it. They had to save Tali. The sword slid through it like butter and the chain clattered to the ground.

"At last," Shemiazaz said in a throaty voice and cackled.

Ginny turned to see the Alliance had torn through the reanimated bodies of the golems and her father rose into the air.

"You cannot defeat me." Jacob laughed and Ginny froze, a warning rising in the back of her mind. She couldn't remember what was wrong, but the feeling devoured her. Something was terribly wrong.

"We'll see about that," Jared said, speeding towards them. Jacob took a few steps to meet him. Jared pulled back his sword, then plunged it into Jacob. But something was off. The sword hit Jacob with a bell-like sound, stopped, then shattered. Jared's face was frozen in shock and he was completely unarmed, then Jacob stabbed him in the chest.

"No!" Ginny and Jesse both called out. Then she remembered. Her blood was protecting Jacob. This was all her fault. Jared fell to the ground and didn't move.

"I can still stop you," Grace said, landing in front of Jacob.

"No, you will be dealing with me, you overgrown bird," Shemiazaz shouted.

The two of them shot into the air. They moved so fast as they battled it was almost impossible to follow them.

"You'll have to deal with us," Jesse said. The members had reached where they stood. Jacob strode forward, a sickening smile on his face.

"Ginny," Aiden hissed from Tali's side. "You have to help me."

Ginny hurried over, Lionel meeting them with tears in

his eyes. Aiden handed her his scribe and she took it, praying this would work.

"You know what you're doing?" Lionel asked.

"Ginny's the strongest healer I know," Aiden answered.

Lionel nodded and Ginny concentrated on the healing sigil, writing it over and over again on Tali's skin doing her best to ignore the sounds of fighting around them and focus only on saving Tali.

"It's working," Tali gasped out, the color returning to her face. Ginny let out a ragged sigh.

Marta rushed them, beating Aiden and Lionel back with a club. She grabbed Ginny's arm and yanked her, pulling her towards the water. She snatched her hand, pulling on the skin until her cut bled fresh again. She chanted in a foreign tongue and Ginny watched in horror as thousands of writhing shapes streamed towards them from under the deceptive depths of the black water. They were demons, distorted creatures with fanged teeth and talons and scales. They rose up between the two worlds, twisting in the water, eager greed lighting up their black eyes. Marta was calling them into our realm and would use Ginny's blood to summon them. Ginny reeled, an army this massive would destroy the Alliance and countless others. She couldn't let them enter. She yanked on her arm, but Marta had it in a vice-like grip. She couldn't stop her.

My blood, my intention. The thought surged through her head.

She looked at Marta and shouted, "I close this portal. No more will it be a door between worlds. I close this door."

Marta stopped and stared at her, unsure. Ginny plunged her hand into the water.

A white cloud filled the lake, pushing the demon army back where they came from, deep into the depths. The entire lake flashed white, then cleared as if nothing had ever happened. Ripples flowed around Ginny's hand as the water lapped at the shore. The portal was gone.

With a cry of rage, Marta reached out and wrapped steel fingers around Ginny's throat. She couldn't breathe and she clawed at Marta's hands to no avail. The little bit of training she had gotten fled her mind in her panic. Black crowded her vision, and she felt faint. She fell to her knees.

Then she was released. She gulped down air, coughing and eyes streaming. Aiden stood above her and gave her a small smile, his tonfa in his hand. "Are you okay?"

She nodded, rubbing her sore throat. Marta lay on her side, unconscious, slumped over a black bag. Ginny turned to Aiden. "You saved me."

"Now we have to save the others."

Ginny turned and saw the Alliance had surrounded Jacob, but Jacob had the upper hand. Their weapons couldn't hurt him. She rushed over to where Tali stood with her father, where they had left them on the beach.

"He's using my blood to protect himself from Alliance weapons," she explained.

"This will stop him," Aiden said, holding up Redeemer.

"It's too dangerous." Ginny shook her head. "I have a plan."

Just like with the portal, it was her blood. Her intention mattered.

Isaac charged Jacob, parrying with him. He was a master swordsman, but that sword was as useless as a toothpick right now, and Jacob knew it. Isaac went for a strike, his sword shattering. Jacob swung wide, slicing his throat. Isaac's hands flew to his neck, even as he fell. Isaiah screamed and ran at Jacob, but Jacob opened his arms wide and let Isaiah hit him. Weaponless and in shock, Isaiah was helpless as Jacob stabbed him clean through. He joined his brother on the beach.

Ginny couldn't breathe. This couldn't be happening. Not to the brothers. The brothers were kind and good and strong. They didn't deserve to die. She staggered a step backwards. They couldn't die. She had to do something. She found her footing and raced forward.

She was directly behind Jacob now. She could see a sort of shimmering aura around him. Her blood protection. Her blood, her intention, she repeated in her head. *My blood will not keep him safe. My blood will not protect him.* She concentrated on these words, repeating them like a mantra, willing them to be true. Jacob's dagger lay discarded on the sand and she picked it up. She watched as a hole emerged in the shimmer around him and aimed for that spot. She stepped into the strike, burying the dagger to the hilt, right through Jacob's heart.

He gasped, then a searing pain overtook Ginny, starting at her wrist where the partial sigil was drawn. *Bound in life, in death, eternal.* The words echoed through her head before blackness engulfed her.

Chapter 28

Aiden gasped for air as he watched Ginny collapse just after Jacob did. He called out her name even though his ears were ringing. A lightning bolt shot through the sky and he felt more than heard the crack of thunder that followed it. Looking up, he saw Shemiazaz fly out of sight, and Grace lit down in front of his daughter, turning her onto her back. Aiden raced towards them.

"Ginny," Aiden murmured, falling to his knees. Grace brushed the hair from her face. "Is she dead?" Aiden asked before he could stop himself.

"No," Grace said quietly. "Just a little lost."

"You have to help her."

Grace nodded, placing a hand on her heart. "You didn't choose this. You didn't choose to be bonded. You can choose now. Your intention matters. Fight off the mark."

Her brow furrowed and her hand twitched. Aiden watched her closely. This couldn't be happening. First Jared, then Tali, then the brothers, now Ginny, lying there looking so helpless. He wasn't ready for this. His heart ached as sweat dripped down his neck.

"Your intention matters. Choose."

Black blood poured out of the cut in her hand and a golden shimmer appeared where the black mark on her wrist was. It glowed brightly, erasing the mark. Color returned to her face and she took a deep breath, opening her eyes.

"Welcome back," Grace said with a smile. She returned it shyly, sitting up.

"Are you okay?" Aiden asked, pulling her into a hug.

"I'm just fine."

"What happened?"

"A bonding ritual," Grace said. "One of the Infernal Rituals because it ties two people in life and death. Ginny didn't participate of her own free will, so it wasn't upheld."

"Thank God for that," Aiden said in a rush.

"Thanks for helping me," Ginny said to Grace. "What happened to Jacob?"

"You stopped him," Aiden answered, pointing at the dead body.

"And his father?"

"I struck him out of the sky. I had to get to you." He looked down and rubbed his neck. "But now he's free."

"What are we going to do?" Ginny asked.

"We'll find him and stop him. He can't use the portal now to bring over his demon army. That was smart thinking on your part, Ginny." Grace smiled proudly.

"Can demons be brought over another way?"

"They can be summoned. Though he won't be able to summon all of them at once, even as powerful as he is," Grace said.

"You know him well," she said softly.

"Yes, we came here together."

Ginny nodded and went to say more, but stopped. She looked at Aiden.

"I'm glad you're okay." He meant those words more than he could say. That terrible moment when she fell, he realized something. He couldn't live without her. Never had he felt this way before. His heart pounded just looking at her.

"I am too. I wasn't ready for goodbyes." Her eyes watered.

"Of course." He reached out and squeezed her shoulder. They shared a look before he stood and went to check on the others.

He found Jackson on the beach. His eyes were rimmed with red.

"We lost three good men today."

Aiden nodded, clearing his throat. The brothers had helped him in so many ways. Training him, showing him kindness always, their gifts on his mission, the ring that had helped him find Ginny. He could never thank them enough, and now he would never have the chance to. His chest felt heavy and the tears came freely.

"Isaac and Isaiah will be missed," Jackson said, putting his arm around Aiden's shoulders. Aiden nodded. They would be greatly missed.

Chapter 29

Ginny blushed as she stood next to her dad, unsure of what to say. There were so many things she wanted to say. Why did he leave? She missed him. He was there the whole time. And she didn't even know how she felt. Anger at his absence, joy at being reunited, confusion that he'd secretly been around anyway. She finally met his gaze.

"You must be confused," he said quietly, rubbing his neck.

"Yes," she said with a laugh. "That's a good place to start. You were there all along. Why did you even leave?"

"It's complicated."

"Try me."

"You were in danger with me around. At first, I just came here to check on you. Just once. But do you remember the first time we met?"

She nodded, a dim memory forming.

"You and Pat came into Lucky's, and you were crying. And well, Pat looked so helpless I had to do something. So I bought you guys milkshakes and we talked. And I had to keep seeing you after that. I wanted to stay away, but I just couldn't."

"You put us through so much pain. Not just me, but mom too. She never got over you leaving. And then you

137

didn't really leave, did you? I wish you would've just stayed."

"I've made many mistakes." He looked down at the ground, frowning. "I thought I was doing what was right. I wanted to keep you both safe."

"I was always at risk for danger. That didn't change when you left."

"You would have been in more danger." He looked into her eyes, pleading for her to understand.

She stuck her chin out and met his gaze. "Well, I'm better equipped to handle it now and up to the challenge."

He stared at her open-mouthed. "I don't know what to say."

"Say you'll come home with me?" her voice rose up in question.

"That's up to your mother," he said sheepishly.

"Ask her. That's all I ask."

He swallowed hard, but nodded.

She kicked at the ground. "I don't even know what to call you."

"What do you want to call me?"

"Dad," she answered honestly.

"Dad it is then." He smiled and opened his arms. She rushed into them.

"I missed you."

He kissed her hair. "I'm here now."

"That better be a promise."

They rejoined the others and Ginny felt a wave of grief wash over her. Jesse was sobbing, his wails filling the air as people took away the bodies. Samson was trying to console him, but was grieving himself. Jesse's cries were like a stab in the heart. No one had a dry eye. A pang opened up in her chest as she remembered shared smiles and words. Jared had always been so kind to her in Bend, so thoughtful. And the brothers had truly welcomed her to the Alliance and given her those wonderful gifts. Three beautiful souls were gone, just like that. The tears rolled down her face. She didn't bother to wipe them away.

After the clean-up crew arrived to take care of the bodies, everyone got back into the SUVs, drained and subdued. It was an odd feeling, to know the normal world had no idea what had just happened when it was so monumental. People would visit this lake and never know the truth. That three men had given everything to stop Jacob, that Jacob was now dead, or that the demon Shemiazaz was free and roaming the world. But she would never forget.

Grace put a hand on her knee and the overwhelming grief subsided. She found hope. Jacob was gone, and they wouldn't rest until they found his father. And her dad was back in her life. And she couldn't forget that Aiden was beside her. She had wished for her father for so long, it was like a dream come true that he was here now. Grace fidgeted with his collar and constantly ran a hand through his curls. They were dropping them off at Ginny's house. Her mom had just gotten home from Bend.

"I've never seen a nervous angel before." She laughed as he flushed.

"It's been a long time since I've seen your mother." His voice was a little too high.

"I don't think you have to worry."

"What do you know? You're not an adult."

She glanced at Aiden. She knew something about it. "Let me go in first," she said as they pulled up.

He nodded gratefully.

She bounded up the steps and threw the door open. "Mom?"

"Oh my God, Ginny! Are you alright? I've been crazy with worry," Helena said, running up to meet Ginny in the hallway.

"Yes, I promise. I'm fine. And I have great news for you." She paused for dramatic effect. "Dad's home."

Helena stared at her blankly.

"Didn't you hear me?"

"He's here? Right now? You have to be joking?"

"Joking? Aren't you happy?"

"Happy? Have you seen my hair? And these jeans?

I'm not ready to meet him. I only just got in. I haven't changed yet."

"He's not going to care about your jeans, mom. He's beside himself waiting to meet you."

"It's been years, dear. Fine for him, he doesn't age, but it's a different story for me."

"Mom, you look great. Now the love of your life is waiting outside to meet you again. Are you going to make him wait?"

"Yes?"

The door opened and Helena's mouth fell open as Grace entered.

"I love the hair and the jeans," he said shyly.

"Oh, stop." Tears sprang into her eyes.

He walked past Ginny and whispered in Helena's ear. Tears fell down her cheeks, but she had the biggest smile Ginny had ever seen. She nodded.

"Ginny, I have something to ask you." He stopped short, swallowing.

"Go on."

"I want to stay with you guys for a while. Get to know you again and be a family. What do you say?"

"It's about time." She ran over to hug them both.

Chapter 30

Ari stared at his dinner, listening to his father entertain Benedict. The other New York members were out, so they spoke freely. Well, more freely.

"So, it was my first time fighting an actual demon. We had just finished training. And the demon summoned was seven feet tall. Jackson and Lionel were dealing with the warlocks who had summoned it, having a hell of a time. So I was all alone, facing this beast with a scorpion tail that was even taller than it was and six arms. I'm fighting like crazy as it slashes at me with its claws. Finally, I gut the thing, but not before it sticks me with its tail. The poison was so venomous I passed out before I even fell, but the boys healed me, and I got a good story out of it. Cool scar too."

"Indeed," Benedict said, taking a bite of steak with relish.

"But enough of me and my war stories, let's move on to more important matters."

Ari pushed his still fully laden plate away and placed his elbows on the table, pressing his hands together before him.

"Our ally is making moves to place himself in power. He guarantees us a place in the new world order."

Benedict raised a brow. "And how exactly does he

promise this? It won't be easy to remove our public offices."

"With an army worthy of change. We are also working to exact change from within when the time is right. That's where you come in. With your standing, you can sway many to our cause."

Benedict took a bite. "I need more than just words to put myself out there."

Gideon pushed his plate away, steepling his fingers. "First, we conquer the Alliance, then the world."

"Those are lofty words," Benedict said between bites, his mouth full.

"They are more than words, I assure you."

He held up his fork. "Say I throw my lot in with you...."

"You'll have a new seat in government. More than just a chapter head."

Benedict smiled, and Ari breathed easier.

"Well, shall we retire to the sitting room?" Benedict asked, setting down his fork and knife.

They all rose and left the room. But Ari's father's phone rang.

"I'll meet you in there."

Ari waited while his father answered the phone.

"What do you mean?" his father exploded. "What are you talking about? Explain yourself."

Ari watched his father, whose face changed to a deep red as he listened.

"When did this happen? Are you absolutely sure?" He paused, a vein pulsing in his forehead. "We'll discuss this later."

"What happened?" Ari asked in a hush as his father stared at his phone.

"Jacob is dead."

"How is that possible?"

"It's all over the Alliance. He was killed by Ginny of all people."

"What do we do?"

"Use this to our means."

Ari raked a hand through his hair. *This situation was impossible.* "How?"

His father took a calming breath. "Aiden's related to Jacob. We tout him as Jacob's successor. With Jackson's known support of the boy, we just need to say the current Council is corrupt, working for Jacob's heir. Then we take the Council back and enact our plans. Come, we need to talk."

"What about Benedict?"

"He will approve of our new plans. Come."

Ari followed his father, a nervous knot forming in his stomach.

Chapter 31

Tali had almost died and it put things in perspective. When she'd been lying there in agony, demon poison coursing through her veins, she kept seeing Pat's face at Lucky's the last time she had seen him. The smile that lit up his eyes as he had seen her come in and the confusion and hurt that painted his face when she had left without an explanation. Tali had been so focused—no, obsessed—with the idea of being with Aiden, she had mistreated an awesome guy who she liked being with. She had refused to give Pat a second thought and now realized what a mistake she had made.

But could she fix this mistake? She had survived and that meant she had to try. She picked up her phone and called Pat.

"Hi," his voice held no warmth, and Tali swallowed hard, trying to think of how to proceed.

"I want to talk." Straightforward would be best. "Do you have time today?"

"I guess. I could make some time."

She breathed. "Great. There's a park near me, Ryder Park. Meet me there at noon?"

"I'll find it."

"See you then, Pat."

She hung up, heart pounding. Already his behavior

towards her had changed so greatly. Could she win him back? Is that really what she wanted? She thought now that it was.

Ryder park was where she had colluded with the enemy. She would now reclaim it as the spot where she found her new relationship, her new life. Aiden had been a dream, and such a longstanding one, she had been sure it was real. But it was never real. Not like Pat who actually saw her for who she was. And when she took Aiden out of the equation, she was surprised to find she had feelings for Pat. She could only hope he still had feelings for her.

She took her time in the shower, gathering her thoughts and newfound feelings. She wanted to do this right. She owed Pat her best effort at fixing this. And she needed it for herself as well. When her mind was organized, she finished her shower, taking down and re-braiding her hair and applying makeup. Her favorite lavender blush, pink eyeshadow, and a plum lip. She picked out a pretty outfit and gave herself an approving look in the mirror. Then she headed down to the kitchen for some food.

Aiden was there and she stopped short in the doorway.

"Hey," he said, putting his plate in the sink.

"Hey." She examined her nails. He had said he would never talk to her again, and she would respect that after what she had done.

"Look, I don't want things to always be weird between us. We've been friends for years, and I value that time we had together. What you did was messed up, and you broke our trust—so we can't exactly be like we were before—but I don't want to be awkward and always avoiding each other either."

She looked up. "I don't want that either. But I know what I did was wrong. I won't forget that."

Aiden nodded.

"And I don't want to date you anymore. I've come to realize exactly what it is I want. For so long that was you, and I got confused. But that's all in the past now. I want to be with Pat."

Aiden looked surprised, but nodded again. "I'm happy

for you. Now, if you'll excuse me, I have some things to do."

Tali made brunch with some eggs and fruit. It was hard to concentrate on her meal with the torrent of thoughts pouring through her head about both Aiden and Pat. She would be happy if she could salvage some type of friendship with Aiden. As for Pat, she just hoped it wasn't too late.

The time came to leave, and she found her heart was racing in her chest. She took a couple calming breaths and made her way to the park. She arrived first and sat on the bench, tapping her fingers on her thighs as she waited. The wind rustled through the trees around the park as some neighborhood kids played on the jungle gym. She pulled the collar of her jacket closer around her neck as the swings creaked to her right.

"It's a little chilly today," Pat's voice came from behind her. She turned to face him, but his expression was inscrutable.

She gestured to the bench. "Have a seat."

He obliged, but looked down at the ground, not saying anything. This was fine. She wanted to lead this conversation anyway.

"I was rude the last time we spoke," she began. "I'll tell you why I was rude, and then it's up to you whether you forgive me or not." She took a deep breath. "Ever since I was nine and met him, I had feelings for Aiden. We were inseparable and he meant everything to me. A crush grew into an obsession I'm only now starting to see clearly. When you told me you liked me, I had nowhere to put that. All space was already taken.

"But then I did something reprehensible because I lost sight of what was right in my obsession. Nothing mattered except for him being mine. I realized the mistake I had made and tried to fix it. And in doing so, I almost died. You heard, I'm sure, of that last battle with Jacob."

He nodded. "I heard some from Ginny."

"When I freed Ginny from her bonding spell, Jacob stabbed me with a demon blade. As I lay there dying, I didn't think of Aiden or even of my father. I thought of you, Pat. I thought of your eyes lighting up whenever you saw me, and I thought of your face when I left the last time, and I realized I had feelings for you. Not an obsession, but genuine feelings for you. I want to be with you. I want to try dating and see where that leads. I want that if you still want me, that is."

Pat was quiet for a moment, and Tali could hear her heart beating in her ears. Her nerves twanged and she controlled her breathing to try to calm herself.

Finally, Pat spoke. "I meant what I said. That I really liked you. And that's still true. And I get what you mean about Aiden. I felt a similar way about Ginny before I met you. But I know this is different from that immature crush I held onto. I'd like to give us a try."

Tali let out a sigh of relief and grinned. Pat reached over to hug her. They laughed as they held each other close. Worries and fears slaking off them.

"Let's go on a date," Pat said, pulling away with a big grin on his face.

"Go where?"

"Dinner and a movie?"

"Sounds nice." She smiled shyly at him. This was all new to her.

"Great. I'll pick you up at six."

"I'll text you the address."

They hugged and then left. Tali was excited about their first date, but also nervous. A new feeling for her bubbling in her stomach. Still, she couldn't hide her grin as she walked home.

Chapter 32

A few days later, Ginny entered Alliance house with her Dad in tow. He was there to discuss a plan to find and capture Shemiazaz with the Council. Ginny went to go find Aiden. She figured they could do some school work together. She wandered into the living room. Suddenly she was struck by the memory of the brothers playing a video game. Isaac had won a wrestling match with Isaiah by tickling him. Ginny smiled until she was hit with the memory that they were both gone.

She sat down on the loveseat, trying to breathe deeply to steady herself. She'd never see them again, and she had herself to blame. It'd been her blood, blood she just gave up to Jacob, which had caused their deaths. Her heart ached fiercely as she saw their smiling faces in her mind. They had always been so kind to her, even giving her and Aiden those gifts on their mission. Tears came unbidden, slipping down her cheeks. A sob escaped her and she clapped a hand over her mouth, but the tears didn't stop. The house was so empty without them and their laughter and smiles.

"It gets easier." Her dad's voice was soft as he entered the room. "Remembering them I mean."

She swiped her eyes and turned to face him. "But they died because of me." A sound escaped her again.

"It's no one's fault but Jacob's." He sat next to her and pulled her into his arms. "You were under the effect of a rather unfortunate ritual. A ritual that Jacob forced upon you. And it was Jacob who murdered them."

She felt herself calming, a soothing feeling overtaking her. She sighed and snuggled against his chest.

"You did nothing wrong," he cooed. "And you stopped Jacob from hurting anyone else. Don't forget that."

"I wish I had stopped him sooner."

"Things happen for a reason. We just don't always understand that reason."

"They were just such beautiful people..." she trailed off.

"And they still are. They left a beautiful legacy behind them as well."

"I'll never forget them."

Her dad smiled at her. "That's wonderful. Grief is just love that has no place to go."

She rested her head against his chest again, deep in thought as he played with her hair. "We lost Jared too. I didn't know him as well, but he was always thoughtful of others. It must be so hard for Jesse."

"Yes. It's always hard to lose someone you love."

"I know you speak from experience. Sorry."

"No need to be sorry. Loving someone is never something to be sorry about, even when goodbyes are painful. We learn so much from them and we have so many wonderful memories to cherish."

She sighed. "But poor Jesse is even away from home."

"He has Samson and is in a place that won't always remind him of what he's lost. That helps in the beginning."

"I wish I could do something for him."

"Well, everyone grieves in different ways, so there's no one right way to approach helping him. Just be a loving person to him. That's the best you can do."

"You're right. I know I can't make him feel better. He needs to grieve. I just want to support him."

He hugged her closer. "How did I end up with such a wonderful daughter?"

"Good genes?"

They laughed, and Ginny felt lighter. She was grieving the loss of her friends, but the world would go on. She would just do her best to honor them. "Thanks for making me feel better."

"Just glad I could help." He kissed her hair. "Now don't you have some homework to do?"

"Yes," she said with a sigh. She sat up and stretched.

"We have some more things to discuss, including Tali's punishment. I'll come get you when I'm done."

"Okay."

She left. On her way to Aiden's room, she bumped into Tali.

"Hey," Ginny said with a smile, waiting to see how Tali would receive it.

"Hi," Tali's smile was shy. They hadn't really spoken since Tali almost died for Ginny.

"How are you? Feeling fine?" Ginny tucked a piece of her hair behind her ear.

"Oh, yeah. Just fine. Thanks to you really." She looked down.

She reached out her hand and placed it on Tali's arm. "No, you're the one who broke the bond. I don't know what would have happened if you didn't. Just the end of the world. You know, the usual." Ginny laughed as Tali blushed.

Tali kept her eyes down. "It was my fault in the first place."

"I'm just glad you knew what to do to free me. That's what matters." And Ginny meant it. Aiden and Jackson had explained the bonding ritual to her and Tali's part in it all. And sure, what Tali had done in the first place was wrong, but she'd be a mindless slave if it wasn't for her doing the right thing in the end. What Tali had done was brave and had almost cost Tali her life. Tali had even wanted to die from her guilt. Ginny was glad that hadn't happened. "Look, I know we've been through a lot. It would be nice if we had a clean start with each other."

Tali looked up at her. "I think I could do that." When Tali smiled, it was clear it was genuine.

"Great. I'm off to find Aiden to do our homework. We're so behind."

"Let me know if you need help with anything."

"Thanks."

Ginny found Aiden in his room listening to music. "Hey," she said, knocking on the open door.

"Hello stranger. What gives me the pleasure of your company?"

"Our mutual need to do homework so we don't become dropouts."

He made a face. "But what if I want to drop out?"

"I think Jackson would kill you."

He laughed. "Good point."

They worked steadily until her dad came to get her, putting a dent in the pile of papers they had to turn in. The break from school had been nice, but Ginny wasn't sure she appreciated the tradeoff of so much work to do now. Still the mission had been important. She hugged Aiden goodbye and joined her dad in the hallway.

"I'll meet you at the car. I want to say bye to Jesse."

"Okay, sweetie." Her dad's smile was brilliant.

She made her way down the hall to the guest quarters, butterflies in her stomach. She didn't know what to say to him exactly, but she had to say something. She had to try. She knocked lightly on his door.

After a few nerve wracking minutes, he opened the door. The change was almost a shock to her, but she schooled her face and smiled warmly at him. His eyes were red, rimmed with dark circles. His face was pale and drawn and his hair was unkempt.

"I wanted to stop by and see you," she began, unsure of what to say next.

"Thanks for stopping by." His voice was deadpan, and Ginny bit her lip.

"I know there's nothing I can say to make things better right now. I just wanted you to know I'm your friend. And if I can do anything for you, I will."

He closed his eyes for a moment before looking her in the eyes. "It's just so hard."

She reached out and grabbed his hand. "I can only imagine."

"I wake up thinking he's just down the hall, and then

reality hits me, and I lose him all over again." Tears trickled down his hollow cheeks. He probably wasn't eating.

"I'm so sorry."

"I just don't know what to do."

She squeezed his hand. "I'm no expert, but I think you take it one moment at a time. Do small things for yourself, like eating and sleeping. Distract yourself with things you usually enjoy, even if you don't enjoy them right now. And remember you're not alone in this. You have friends. Do you have my number? You can text me any time."

"Yes, I have it. Thanks."

"I meant it. Any time."

He gave her a watery smile. "Thanks for stopping by." This time it sounded like he meant it.

"Of course. I'll come see you again soon."

She gave him a hug, then left. She couldn't help but feel worried about him. It was right of her to stop by.

Chapter 33

Shemiazaz had landed just outside of Seoul when Grace had blasted him out of the sky. And landing on a mountain had hurt. Some trees had slowed his fall, their cracking trunks piercing him deep. He may not be able to die from these grave injuries, but that didn't mean he didn't feel them. He cursed Grace as he plucked slivers and chunks of tree from his wounds.

Then there was getting back to the portal. He had a demon army to summon. His idiot of a son should have summoned them before the Alliance came, but he'd been lovestruck and only concerned with bonding with Ginny permanently. Still he'd been clever enough to use her blood as a shield against the Alliance. An idea that appealed to Shemiazaz himself. Grace's blood would be powerful enough to work.

He had no time to lose, so he changed into mortal form, swiping his blond hair behind his ear. He made his way down the mountain to a street where he hailed a cab. First he had to get to the airport a couple of hours away. That would give him enough time to recover and plan. When he arrived in Incheon, he went to work convincing some airline employee to purchase his ticket back to the United States and to let him onboard without identification. He'd taken a suit off a man in the bathroom and taken care of his unruly blond hair before he reached the ticket line. Grace had no idea of knowing exactly where he was yet, and he wouldn't dare strike him out of the sky with so many passengers on board if he was discovered. Around fifteen hours later, Shemiazaz was landing and finding a ride back to the lake house his son had owned. He needed that portal. He would be even more powerful with his army. Then, if he couldn't convince Aiden to help him with the persuasion of granting him angelborn abilities, he'd be able to do so by force. He could easily overwhelm the Alliance force in Lockewood and take Aiden and the sword to free his brothers.

When he arrived in town, twilight was drawing near. The sky was a deep blue with streaks of crimson clouds close to the horizon. Stars were beginning to peek out and a wind rustled the lake waters. Shemiazaz strolled towards the lake when he noticed a man hiding in the tree line at the edge of the beach. He was hunched over, sitting at the base of a tree in the gathering dark. Shemiazaz sent his mind into the man's.

It was Mordecai, lost and mourning his master Jacob. Something glowed dully in the light, Jacob's dagger.

"Come to me," Shemiazaz ordered the bedraggled man. Mordecai tugged at his wispy beard and scrambled up and lumbered to where Shemiazaz stood by the water. "You serve me now as you did my son."

Mordecai's eyes gleamed. "Master," he whispered.

"Give me the dagger and hold out your hand."

Mordecai obliged. Shemiazaz cut deep into Mordecai's palm, ignoring his cry of pain.

"I summon my demon children. Come forth unto this realm and join me in glory," he said, holding Mordecai's bleeding hand over the water. The blood dripped, swirling in the lapping water, but nothing happened. Shemiazaz repeated his summons to no avail. Anger simmered in his stomach. The portal wasn't working. "Damn," he hissed, dropping Mordecai's hand.

"What now, master?" Mordecai asked, holding his hand to his chest. It would soon be healed.

"We do this the old-fashioned way."

Chapter 34

Aiden felt like he was flying. He jumped high into the air, his body tingling in response. Power surged through him. He could do anything. He did a backflip, landing gracefully, and put his hand on the ground. Grass tickled his fingers, spongy beneath his hand. He was in a field, long grass and wildflowers stretching before him. The wind ruffled his hair, cooling his face. He had never felt energy like this before, as if his whole body thrummed. He laughed.

"It can always be like this." A voice rang low and raspy in his ear. He snapped his head around, looking for the source of the voice. There was no one there. "Power and strength like you've only imagined," the voice continued. "You can have it, always."

"Who are you?"

"One who would call you a friend."

"If you're a friend, show yourself to me."

A man approached him in the distance. Tall with shining

blond hair and a devious grin. There seemed something familiar about him, but Aiden couldn't place him from anywhere. The hairs rose on the back of his neck. This man was powerful, if he was even a man at all. Aiden had to be careful.

Aiden stood, hands forming fists at his side. "Do I know you?"

"We've met, but not been introduced." Again the man leered at Aiden, and Aiden's hands grew clammy. Something wasn't right about this stranger.

"Tell me your name."

"I am called Shemiazaz." The corner of the man's lip turned up into a mischievous snarl. Aiden's heart skipped a beat and he faltered, unsure of what to say. "I have a proposition for you."

His nails dug into his palms. "What could you possibly want? You're free now."

"I am, yes. But my brothers are not. When we swore to go against God, they were punished alongside of me. I wish to grant them their freedom as well."

"And wage your own war."

His face hardened. "I do not create war."

"But you would fight one."

"I make no promises. It is a nasty habit."

Aiden stood, brushing the grass off his hands. "You'd make me one to get what you want."

Shemiazaz smiled again. "It is not a promise, more like a guarantee. And it would get us what we both want."

"I don't want anything." Aiden waved his hand in the air.

"Not even to be angelborn?" Shemiazaz arched a brow.

Aiden scoffed. "Even if I did, you couldn't make that happen."

The corner of Shemiazaz's mouth curled up. "Ginny could. And I can tell you how."

Aiden paused. "She's powerful, but not that powerful."

"It's blood magic. It would transform you. I know the ritual. I could show you. All you would need is her blood."

"Blood magic?"

"It is not inherently evil."

Aiden shook his head hard. Jackson had always warned

them against this. "I couldn't."

"Feel the power surging through you. It could be like this, always."

"But at what cost?"

"Wield your sword and free my brothers."

"And unleash that many fallen angels onto the world?"

Shemiazaz shrugged. Still he wore that insufferable look, and it reminded Aiden of Jacob. He clenched his jaw. He felt another surge of power as he regarded Shemiazaz. He closed his eyes for a moment, savoring the feeling.

"This could be yours, always." The words echoed in his head.

When he opened his eyes, he was staring up at the ceiling of his room. Grey light filtered in through the curtains. That delicious feeling had vanished, leaving him hollow. He sighed and rolled over, trying to regain sleep. After a few, futile minutes, he gave up.

Stepping into the shower, the dream wouldn't leave his mind. How exhilarating he had felt, how alive, played over and over again in his mind. He had felt so strong, so vibrant, so capable. But at what cost? The dream came crashing down again.

Perdition's most powerful demon was trying to trick him. He recoiled from the thought, turning the tap to cold and grabbing his shampoo. He could never accept Shemiazaz's help. And blood magic was dark and dangerous. Jackson refused to teach his kids that subject for a reason. It was a dirty word for dirty deeds. Things demons did. Aiden could have no part of that. Even if he did want to be angel-born.

And he did. He couldn't lie to himself. It had been his greatest wish since he had joined the Alliance at ten years old. Always the outsider, the outcast. Always put down for being *just a human.* He would have their powers with sigils—no more weak casting—have their healing powers, and be a stronger fighter. Shemiazaz said he just needed Ginny's blood. Maybe he didn't need Shemiazaz to get what he wanted. But would Ginny agree to help him? With all the negative connotations against blood magic, he wasn't sure. Still, they could figure it out together. *Did he dare ask her?* His confidence faltered as he stepped back under the cold water.

What if she just sees it as evil? Or she just doesn't want to help him? His limbs tingled, remembering the effects of the dream. It was intoxicating. But he had to stop. It was time to wake up and get on with this day. He gave his head a shake and quickly finished his shower.

Light was filling his room as he threw on some clothes. His mood was tempestuous as he slammed the drawers home. He needed to do something, maybe go for a walk to clear his head. He pounded downstairs, about to turn for the veranda when he heard harsh voices.

He recognized Gideon's voice right away. "You can't fool us."

Aiden walked behind him, unnoticed for now.

"The Council is corrupt, and we have proof of it. Aiden is Jacob's heir and Aiden will no doubt continue carrying on Jacob's dastardly agenda. And you have always pandered to the boy. You are no longer fit to run this Council."

"Hear, hear," others cried out. Aiden's face flushed with heat.

"There are rumors that you, Gideon, were the one working with Jacob. Not Aiden," Jackson replied coolly.

"Do you always listen to rumors?" Gideon scoffed.

"You come here with nothing but a rumor yourself and expect to be heard. From day one, Aiden has done everything he could to stop Jacob at every juncture and has successfully stopped his plans. This Council is not corrupt."

Gideon smirked. "Let's have a vote on that then, shall we?"

"Gather the members for a noon meeting," Jackson conceded.

Gideon twirled and walked straight into Aiden, pulling a face of disdain. "It's you, boy. Get out of my way."

He waved his hand in Aiden's face, but Aiden refused to budge, staring off to the side. With a huff, Gideon finally stepped around Aiden, knocking into him with his shoulder. Aiden laughed.

"Where is my son?" Gideon shouted, striding away.

Aiden scowled. They were calling a meeting, and Gideon was trying to use Aiden to get his Council seat back. And if rumors were true, Gideon would be the one carrying on Jacob's work. A world where angelborn would be elite over the paltry humans. It was enough to turn Aiden's stomach.

"Never mind him," Jackson said quietly as he placed his hand on Aiden's shoulder.

"You could lose the Council seat because of me."

"Not because of you. You have not done anything wrong. I want you to understand that."

"I know. It's just we can't let Gideon have power again. Not with what he wants to do."

"We will not." Jackson smiled at him for a moment. "There is breakfast still in the kitchen." Of course, a reminder to eat. Aiden nodded and strolled towards the kitchen. Ginny leaned against the counter, nibbling on toast with jelly.

Aiden zeroed in on the plates of eggs and bacon. "There's going to be a meeting," he began nonchalantly. "Gideon wants the Council kicked off for supporting Jacob's heir."

She put the toast down and crossed her arms. "What?"

"Apparently, I plan on continuing Jacob's plans."

"I thought that's what Gideon was doing."

"Anyway, there will be a vote. Pretty exciting I guess." He shoveled a forkful into his mouth. This whole situation was ludicrous.

"I should tell my dad what they're up to. He'd stop them."

"Is he allowed to interfere?"

"He stopped them from kicking you out and they lost their seats in the first place."

Aiden recalled when Gideon had tried to eject him

from the Alliance. Jacob had kidnapped Pat and the Council had refused to rescue him, going against their sacred mandate to protect humans from demonkind. All to punish Ginny of course. Aiden and Ginny had gone on their own to save Pat. And Aiden got in big trouble for it. Right when he was about to be expelled from the Alliance, Grace had shown up and removed Gideon and Darius from the Council instead, instating Jackson and Lionel in their place.

"Maybe that would be a good idea."

Ginny pulled out her phone and started texting. Aiden ate methodically, mind preoccupied with the thoughts that still lingered from his dream. *Would Ginny help him if he asked her? Could he even do that?* He scowled into his eggs.

"Hey," Ginny said, coming up to him. "We won't let Gideon win."

"He still has a lot of power. Even without his seat."

She checked her phone before frowning. "It'll work out," she said, but she seemed distracted.

"What's wrong?"

"It's just my dad. I think he's still out, searching for Shemiazaz."

"He might not be able to help us." The realization hit Aiden. He put down his fork.

"That doesn't mean anything."

Aiden got up to throw the rest of his breakfast away, no longer hungry.

"I mean, who would listen to Gideon anyway? This whole thing is unbelievable."

Aiden sighed. "A lot of people, actually. He has a lot of clout."

"But that doesn't even make sense. You working for Jacob? We've just spent months doing everything we could to stop him."

"Gideon isn't the only member who wants me out. This is the perfect chance to get what they want. People will take advantage of that."

Ginny bit her lip as she regarded him. He sighed, wanting to take away her worries, even though he felt them himself keenly.

"It's not hopeless," he finally managed to say. "Not

everyone agrees with Gideon. Let's just wait and see what happens."

She gave him a small smile and nodded. They had a couple hours till the meeting, but they were too distracted to do more than watch a couple movies. They sat next to each other on the couch, not talking much. For once, Aiden was relieved for that as he tried to untangle his own worries and fears. What exactly was Gideon capable of? Would Aiden really be forced to leave the Alliance, after all? He couldn't rely on Grace saving him this time. Shemiazaz had to be captured and now. Grace couldn't forsake his duties for Aiden's sake. He swallowed hard.

Tali walked into the living room with Pat. Aiden raised a brow. She was on house arrest for what she had done, but that didn't mean she couldn't have visitors apparently.

"PJs!" Ginny exclaimed, jumping up to give her best friend a hug. Aiden exchanged a look with Tali. "What are you doing here?"

"Just hanging out with Tali."

"Of course." She smiled. "Well, we're just watching a movie, but you're welcome to join."

Pat and Tali sat in a loveseat to the side, talking quietly. Aiden tapped his fingers against his thigh, trying to combat his urge to grab Ginny's hand.

The tension had lessened, but it was still there. And, in Aiden, it grew as the time for the meeting approached. Ginny kept checking her phone, so Aiden knew she was worried too. Finally, the time came.

"Time to go," Aiden said, standing. He ran a hand through his hair. Ginny stood without a word.

"Wait here," Tali said to Pat, giving his arm a squeeze.

The three of them made their way to the assembly room. Everyone had gathered, including Samson and Jesse. Jesse's head hung low as he slumped in his seat, staring at a spot on the floor, unmoving. There were dark circles around his eyes, and he seemed oblivious to the world around him.

They took seats in the back. The room was pretty filled up, and Aiden didn't want to be on display when he knew Gideon would be accusing him of being Jacob's heir and accomplice.

Gideon strutted into the room, nose in the air. His son and the rest of his entourage followed, full of smug smirks. Jackson looked like he was struggling not to roll his eyes.

"This Council had a request to hold this meeting, and has graciously allowed it," Jackson began. "We were under no obligation to do so, but for the sake of getting the truth heard, the Council agreed—"

"And the truth," Gideon interrupted, "is that this Council is corrupt."

Shouts filled the room.

"You seem to forget," Lionel said dryly, "that you are the one who was disbarred for being corrupt. Not us."

Ethan looked around nervously.

"There is no denying that Aiden King is, in fact, directly related to Jacob. No one has come forward to deny this, because it is the unmitigated truth. And we have every reason to believe he will continue Jacob's nefarious plans. After all, Jacob left him an inheritance. Why do so if they are not aligned?"

"Aiden has been actively impeding Jacob's every move for the last couple of months. Every step he has taken has been solely to stop Jacob's plans from succeeding. It is a joke to say he is continuing on with those plans." Jackson glared at Gideon.

"The security of this Council and, therefore, the Alliance is a joke to you?" Gideon's voice went high.

"Your accusations are a joke. This Council is only in danger from idiots like you."

Lionel coughed, stifling a laugh while Ethan went red in the face. The entire room was silent.

Gideon reared. "How dare you. You've always pandered to that human. The only thing you are showing is your lack of integrity and your bias towards the boy. You are not fit to run this Council."

Shouts of agreement rang out and Aiden's face grew hot. "Then why did the angel himself assign Jackson to the Council while you were disbarred? Do you now claim more integrity than Grace?" he asked loudly.

Gideon sputtered and a murmur went around the

room.

"The angel said you were not fit to sit on this Council. How dare you try to usurp the seat again now."

"I am more worthy than you," Gideon spat out.

"But not more worthy than Jackson. According to Grace of course. This isn't just my opinion."

"Let us put it to a vote," Gideon said, splaying his hands. "Those who think it's time for a new Council, raise your hands."

Half the hands went up.

"It is not a majority vote," Jackson said with a smile.

"We will not be ignored. Until we are heard, we are withdrawing our services to the Alliance."

"So once again you break your sacred oath?" Aiden asked, shaking. *They couldn't do that. This was unheard of.*

Gideon and the others stood. Clearly this had been orchestrated.

Jackson stood also, leaning on the podium before him. "You break your oath again, you are all in danger of being ejected from the Alliance for this. Permanently."

A few hesitated by their seats. Gideon glared at them. "Our demands are simple and easily met."

"This is not how the Alliance works," Lionel said calmly. "You cannot blackmail us into giving you what you want."

"There will be consequences." Jackson promised.

Finally, the last of the traitors was at the door. Gideon smirked at the Council and bowed before leaving.

"I can't believe that bastard," Tali muttered. "That's the most mad I've ever seen my dad."

Everyone was talking at once, it was chaotic.

"They won't get away with this. They should all be kicked out now," Ginny said.

Jackson cleared his throat and spread his hands. "Please come forth and sign this sheet of paper. We need a record of those who did not break their mandate with heaven." Everyone got up and began to line up at the podium.

It was then that the phone on the desk rang. Ginny jumped, then smoothed her hair down, flustered. Jackson answered, his face turning pale before hanging up.

"What's wrong?" Lionel asked.

"That was Shemiazaz. He has summoned us to battle."

Lionel started. "Where?"

"The lake."

"But we have so few," Ethan said, running a hand down his pale face. "How can we win with half our forces gone?"

"We must go regardless," Jackson replied with a sigh. "Shemiazaz must be stopped at all costs." He set his shoulders and announced the mission to the room. "Arm yourselves and rendezvous out front."

Chapter 35

Ginny stared at the members leaving in disbelief. They followed them out of the room in stunned silence and found Pat in the living room.

"What's going on?" he asked, standing. He ruffled his messy blond hair and stared with wide brown eyes.

Aiden and Tali both looked stoic and unreadable. Jackson walked by, his face a studied mask, but he ran a telltale hand through his hair as he passed. He paused to address Tali, then walked away. There was an uncomfortable silence as everyone walked out. Ginny could hardly believe the Alliance had actually split, that Gideon had succeeded in dividing them. All based on a rumor. Sure Aiden was related to Jacob and had inherited the lake house, but it was him who had fought so hard to stop Jacob on their mission. *Why couldn't people see that?*

"I have to tell my dad," Ginny said, pulling out her phone. She walked away to make the call. Her dad agreed to meet them immediately, but he sounded worried. She rejoined the others.

"You better get home," Aiden said to Pat.

Pat stood tall and puffed out his chest. "No way. You guys need help."

"You don't know how to fight demons."

He crossed his arms. "I've been in a fight or two. And

I've seen what demons can do."

"Pat's right," Ginny added. "We need all the people we can get. Give him some weapons.Tali, are you fighting?"

Tali shifted her feet, looking unsure. "Yeah, Jackson said he needed me, but it's dangerous."

Pat put a hand on her arm. "And I want to help keep you all safe. I can't just walk away."

"Are you sure?" Aiden looked him square in the eye, sizing him up.

Pat returned his gaze, unwavering. "One hundred percent."

"Then we should belt up."

They walked down to the gymnasium where Aiden put weapon belts on Ginny and Pat and supplied them with swords and knives. Then Tali and Aiden took care of themselves. Pat looked pale but determined as he took a few practice swings with his sword, the aoiveae blade shining in the light. The blessed metal always gleamed.

"Let's go find the others," Aiden said, zipping up his hoodie.

The others were milling about the cars. The air was brisk, their breath hanging in front of their faces. The end of autumn was upon them, but no one wore coats that would impede their movements. Ginny hugged herself to stay warm, heart beginning to pound. Fighting Jacob had been one thing, but his father was a powerful demon, the most powerful demon. What would they be up against? She shook her head, trying to clear it. There were dozens of members waiting to get into cars, but it wasn't enough. Sure the portal was closed, but Shem could still summon demons. Who knew how many at a time.

Samson walked over, followed by Jesse. "You guys ready?"

"Yes, sir," Pat answered, snapping to attention. Samson regarded him, but he had no idea who Pat was, which was for the best. Who knew what Jackson would think of Pat going. But Ginny had to stifle a laugh at the serious look on Pat's face.

Samson gave him a curt nod. "Be prepared for a lot of demons. I want you guys to work like a team. Fight together and watch each other's backs. That's how you'll succeed."

They all nodded, smiling to each other. They would have looked out for each other, even without his words.

They all climbed into cars and SUVs, avoiding the Council leaders. The long procession of vehicles pulled out and made its way to Lake Locke. A sheen of sweat had broken out across Ginny's neck and she braided her hair to the side to keep it from sticking to her or getting in her face. Her palms were clammy too as she held them against her legs. The car was silent, and it fed her anxiety about what they were about to face.

"Hey, you okay?" Aiden's forehead was creased with worry as he regarded her.

"Just anxious about the fight." She leaned over to rest her head on his shoulder.

He placed a hand on her knee and squeezed. "Your dad will be there."

She sat up, biting her lip. But she had to tell him. "He told me on the phone. He can't kill Shemiazaz without a direct order. He doesn't have free will like us, you know."

Aiden looked surprised, but nodded slowly. "That makes sense, since he's an angel. But he can still help us a great deal."

"I just hope he gets there in time."

"He's an angel. He'll be there."

They arrived and everyone piled out, jumping and swinging their arms to limber up and get warm.

"We fight in lines. Close up any holes you see. Do not let yourself get surrounded," Jackson shouted for everyone to hear. "We do our sacred duty today. No matter what."

He was greeted with cheers, this is what they trained for, what they lived for. And what they would die for if necessary. Ginny shook out her arms and thought of her training, of learning to use her powers in Bend, and grabbed her machete. They marched to the lake where Shemiazaz stood in mortal form. She rolled up her sleeves.

He was beautiful. Golden blond hair and piercing blue eyes that stared at them defiantly. His features reminded Ginny of Jacob, and her stomach turned to see it.

Beside him was Mordecai, looking oddly bold. She was

used to his simpering behavior, but it seemed he had gained confidence along with a new master. Behind them were what could only be a handful of changelings, probably freshly turned, eyes shining black.

This might not be so bad. The thought was fleeting as Shemiazaz raised his hand and sliced his palm. Where his black blood hit the ground, demons began to squirm their way to the surface. They looked like deformed goat people. Some had animal faces and hands, some human but with animal appendages. They screamed, filling the air with an unearthly sound as they entered this realm, and Ginny's hair stood on end with the wrongness of it all. More and more came until the beach was filled with the demons, led by a changeling in black.

"Line up," Samson shouted and everyone moved as one, brandishing their weapons and walking towards the demons.

To her left were Jackson and Jesse. To her right, Aiden, Tali, and Pat. Then members she didn't know. She clenched her jaw, staring down the demon walking towards her. She could do this, she had to.

It raised a demon blade in its right hand, the metal shone a dulled black, marking it as poisonous. Ginny swallowed hard, raising her kopis machete in a clenched hand. It leered at her as it neared. She swung first.

The swords met with a clang that reverberated down her arm. She used both hands to swing again, slashing at the demon as the sounds of battle started and grew riotous around her. The demon attacked her as it stepped forward. She managed to block as she retreated. He swiped his sword at her again and again. She tried to keep her mind clear, to let her body react to the blows naturally, but she was getting winded. Then she made a mistake. She didn't move fast enough and his blade sliced her forearm.

The pain was sharp and she held her cut arm in her hand. The demon laughed its braying laugh. The wound was shallow, but she waited for the demon poison to kick in as she gasped for air. Adrenaline coursed through her as she stared at the cut.

Nothing happened. She blinked, looking for the

twisted lines of poison that should now be snaking outward from the cut. But it was just a cut. Then she remembered. The sigil on her ankle prevented her from being poisoned by anything demonic. Now it was her turn to laugh.

The demon stared at her, unsure and she used that moment to strike. She thrust her blade through its chest. It bleated, then fell to the ground, clutching at its wound.

She pulled her sword out and a noise to her left caught her attention. Jackson was on one knee, a demon blade sticking out of his thigh. He reached up and stabbed the demon facing him, but his face was already drawn and pale. Ginny rushed to him.

He pulled out the sword from his leg, gasping. The wound was a bloody maw, already turning black. Ginny yanked off her scribe and drew the healing sigil as quickly as she could remember it. A line of members formed in front of them, blocking them from the fight while she worked.

Jackson sighed. "Thank you," he mumbled, wiping his brow before standing.

Ginny caught her breath as she surveyed the scene. The Alliance members were fighting hard against these monsters. The discordant sounds of clashing swords rang out across the beach. Ginny heard a scream and whipped around.

Jesse was lying on the ground with a demon blade buried in his stomach. She ran to him.

"Jesse, it's going to be alright," she said, yanking off her scribe again.

Jesse grabbed her hand in his. "No, please don't. It's better if I die."

Tears sprang to Ginny's eyes. "It's not your time to die, Jesse."

He looked up at her pleading with his eyes. "I just want to be with Jared."

"Suicide is not the answer. And it wouldn't be what Jared would want for you."

His brow furrowed. "You just don't understand." His voice was rough, angry.

"You can hate me, Jesse. But I'm healing you," Ginny said, quickly drawing the sigil on his arm before he could protest.

"No!" Jesse screamed as the sigil flashed gold and melted into his skin. "You've ruined everything!" He started sobbing, even as he was being healed.

"Jackson!" Ginny called for him. He would know what to do.

"What's wrong?"

"You need to get Jesse off the field. He can't fight anymore."

"Let me find Samson."

She looked down at him, eyes hot. "I'm sorry you feel this way, Jesse. But I'm not sorry I healed you."

Jesse just covered his face and sobbed.

Another demon came rushing towards her, gnashing its fanged teeth. It didn't have a weapon, so it was easy to dispatch. She plunged the machete into its chest and yanked it back out.

Samson came and took Jesse away, practically carrying him off the beach. Jackson immediately dove back into the fray.

The goat demons kept coming. Her arms grew weary of holding her sword, but she held on. She had to. A demon leapt at her, striking her blade out of the way with its own. She gasped, startled, and barely fended off its next blow. She was in trouble. When it raised its black sword above her she felt a jolt of energy pulse through her. Everything turned gold and the air grew warm and smelled of lightning. A buzzing feeling filled her and surged outwards.

The demon dropped its sword, screaming. Then the beasts around it followed suit. Radiating outwards like a ripple, demons fell, spasming.

"She summoned the Spirit," someone cried out in awe.

Ginny had done this once before when a changeling had tried to kill her mother. She'd never tried to learn how to control this power, since she only knew she had done so successfully if there were demonkind around. But now it had saved her, and served as a reminder that she could fight with more than just her blade. She released the surge of energy and took a deep breath.

The demons died and a cry rose up from the Alliance members. But Shemiazaz wasn't done yet. He spilled more blood on the ground.

This time the demons that crawled forth were mutations of dogs and humans. Fearsome to behold with their canine teeth and powerful, bounding legs. Ginny shuddered as they came forth in wave after wave. The Alliance formed new lines around the corpses already littering the beach.

The dog demons raced towards them, going at impossible speeds. Ginny's heart thumped so hard in her chest she could hear it. She gripped her machete to try to stop the trembling in her hands. Before she knew it, the monsters had reached the men before her, rending and tearing into their flesh as they pounced.

Ginny looked over to see one leap at Aiden who kicked it out of the air. But the demon landed on its hind legs and bounded back for him. Tali was struggling to fight off two demons that were trying to reach Pat. Her blade arced through the air like a gleam of light and Ginny's heart jumped into her throat. Her friends were in trouble and she had to act now.

Screams filled the air and Ginny sheathed her sword. Setting her jaw and her feet, she concentrated on her core. Willing the desperation she felt to turn into a spark to burn within her. It was time to teach these scum a lesson.

Heavenfire always started so small. Just a flame sparking in her belly that she willed into an inferno. It roared up and she channeled the fire through her arms and down her hands. A demon loped towards her, human face set in a leer. It jumped and golden flames shot from Ginny's hands as she let out a scream. The flames surrounded the demon, burning white hot. Ginny willed more to flow from her, sending them from demon to demon until the whole beach looked as if it was burning. But Ginny was gasping for breath. She'd never used so much heavenfire before, and it was draining her quickly. As the last flame died, she fell to one knee. Jackson ran towards her. "Are you okay?" Concern etched his face as he knelt before her.

"I'm just exhausted. I've never killed that many demons before."

"Shemiazaz isn't done yet," he said with a grim look.

She looked up to see Shemiazaz holding his hand out yet again. She couldn't do this alone. The realization hit her hard and tears sprang to her eyes. *Please*, she prayed, *please help us.*

"You are not alone," a voice echoed through her head.

"Ginny!" her father's voice rang out. She turned to see him flying towards her with two other angels. They were a magnificent sight to behold in their angelic forms. At least eight feet tall with huge, shimmering wings that carried them as they held glowing aoiveae swords in their mighty hands. They were ethereal, with shining hair that glinted in the light, Grace's red-gold and the others' gold. And they were dressed for war.

Shemiazaz's demon army was raised behind Ginny. She turned to see hundreds of them, even grotesque humanoid creatures that chilled her blood. But they would be no match for the angels.

The angels held up their hands and heavenfire sprang up around the demon army. Burning so brightly, most had to look away. There wouldn't even be ash to mark their passing. Ginny sighed in relief as the Alliance members cheered.

Some changelings ran towards the members, but a flick of a finger and the fire engulfed them before they made it a few steps. Mordecai began running back, eyes wild, but he too was surrounded. He burned away with a shriek.

"You may stop my army," Shemiazaz growled, striding forward. "But you cannot stop me."

It was true that the angels couldn't kill him, but was there really no way to stop him? The three angels moved as one, shooting a line of heavenfire. The lines blocked him on three sides and Shemiazaz began to laugh. Ginny rushed forward, using her iron will to summon the flame and boxed him off with a line of her own. Shemiazaz was now encased in golden flames. But for how long?

Then Aiden stepped forwards, holding Redeemer.

"The angels may not be able to stop you, but I can."

Without warning, he stepped into the fire. Ginny screamed.

Chapter 36

Aiden knew what he was doing was dangerous, but he had to do it. Shemiazaz had to be stopped. Heavenfire didn't kill everyone, just those more evil than good, like changelings. Who was he to say whether that was true of him or not, but it was a risk he was willing to take. That's what he told himself as he strode into the flames, holding his breath.

Everything burned. The pain was intense and it stripped everything away from his toes to his head. His muscles clenched and a cry tore from him as he forced his feet forward. It felt like something bored into his brain, ferreting out all his secrets and hidden desires, exposing his very soul for all to see. Tears streamed from his eyes as he took another step forward. And suddenly, the pain stopped. He was through the golden flames, gasping for air.

Redeemer grew hot in his hand. Needles of pain seared his skin so that he almost dropped the sword. Shemiazaz stood there, laughing at him. The light from the heavenfire glinting harshly off his eyes, now black. He bared fangs and raised a hand to strike Aiden down.

Aiden lunged forward with no time to think, burying Redeemer in Shemiazaz's chest. It burned so hot Aiden tore his hand away. Shemiazaz howled. Black blood sputtered from his mouth and seeped from his wound. Shemiazaz tried to rip the sword from his chest, but he couldn't bear to touch it. Demons couldn't wield Redeemer. Only humans could.

The walls of heavenfire descended as the angels stepped forward to watch their fallen brother die. Grace put a hand on Aiden's shoulder, tears falling from his golden eyes.

"Did I do the wrong thing?" Aiden asked, worried at the angel's tears.

Grace's voice was filled with melancholy. "That is not why I cry. I mourn his passing as a brother lost. At what he once was and could have been. That is all."

The other angels bowed their heads as the demon died. Aiden walked over to retrieve Redeemer, but yelled out in pain as soon as his skin touched the handle.

"Why does it hurt?" Aiden asked, brows drawn.

"The heavenfire has transformed you. Not only did you pass the test, but your blood has changed. You are now angelborn, born from the fires of Heaven itself," Grace answered with a smile.

Aiden staggered back as Ginny ran forwards. She threw her arms around him and he laughed, holding her close. All the times he had wished to be like the other Alliance members, to have their abilities, to not be shunned as the only human in the entire organization, and now it had come true. He was angelborn, just like them. He picked Ginny up and swung her around with joy.

He put her down, both of them laughing. The other members crowded around them, in awe of the angels.

"These are my brothers, Abdiel and Adriel." Grace said. The two angels smiled and nodded their heads.

The Alliance members bowed, some with their hands over their hearts.

"It was good to see you," Abdiel said to Grace.

"But it is time for us to go," Adriel finished.

Grace clasped their shoulders with a smile before letting go. They flapped their powerful wings and shot up into the sky.

"Did you hear?" Aiden turned to ask Ginny. She raised a brow. "I'm angelborn now. The fire changed me." His grin split wide.

"That's wonderful," she gushed, hugging him again.

"Would you look at that," he said with a laugh.

Ginny pulled away, a quizzical look on her face. Aiden pointed at what he was seeing. It was Tali and Pat, kissing intently as Lionel tried not to watch.

"Oh wow," Ginny said. Aiden walked up to the amorous pair while Ginny followed, leaving Grace to talk to Jackson. He cleared his throat loudly.

They jumped apart, looking guilty.

"He saved my life," Tali said, jutting out her chin.

"Then I owe him my thanks" was Aiden's reply. He grinned and offered his hand to Pat who smiled sheepishly as he took it.

"I'm happy for you," Ginny whispered to Pat, wrapping her arm around his waist. Aiden felt a huge relief. He knew he was fine with the relationship, but hadn't been sure how Ginny would feel about Pat with Tali.

"He really did save my life," Tali said, grabbing Pat's hand, who blushed. "A demon was right about to gut me when he jumped forward and stabbed it in the heart. And with no training." She gave Pat a look of adoration.

"You did a great job," Aiden agreed.

"Well, she saved me, too. More than once. What I did was nothing."

"Not nothing," Tali admonished.

The way they were looking at each other put Aiden a bit on edge. Sure he was happy for them, but it made him want his own special moment with Ginny.

"Ahem," Lionel said behind them. Tali and Pat whipped around to face him. "I think I need to get to know this boy who keeps touching my little girl." He smirked. Tali blushed but smiled.

"Let's give them some privacy," Aiden said, grabbing Ginny's hand and leading her away. It was now or never time. His hands grew clammy, so he let go of Ginny's hand. Clearing his throat, which had suddenly gone dry, he wiped his hands on his jeans while facing her. He needed to get a hold of himself. This couldn't be any worse than fighting demons.

"Can I kiss you?" he blurted out.

"What?" She looked taken aback, and his heart raced.

He took a breath. "I didn't save your life, but I also don't need you to save mine to know I'm in love with you." The words surprised him, and he laughed.

"I don't know what to say," she said, looking at him shyly.

"Say yes. Say that you'll be mine."

"Oh, Aiden. I already am."

She jumped into his arms and they finally kissed, her lips soft against his, but there was an urgency driving them together. A warmth blossomed in his chest as he held her tight, wrapping his fingers around her hair. He had dreamed of this moment and wanted to savor it forever. But after a few intense minutes, they both drew back to catch their breaths. His heart was pounding, but he had never felt so alive. Ginny looked gorgeous as she laughed, her eyes so filled with gold they didn't look brown at all.

"So are we official?" she asked with a sly grin.

"Official?"

"Like boyfriend-girlfriend. Or do you kiss everyone like that?"

"No," he smiled broadly. "We're definitely official."

They held hands and walked back to their friends. Pat and Tali were laughing with each other.

Jackson approached with a stern look on his face. "Who is your friend?"

Aiden swallowed hard. Jackson had finally caught them bringing a human to a demon fight. "This is your new Keeper. Someone needs to watch Redeemer now that I can't."

Jackson looked startled. "You cannot? What do you mean?"

"The heavenfire. I'm angelborn now." He couldn't help but grin.

Jackson clapped him on the arm with a smile. "While I am happy for you, I cannot approve of you bringing a human to fight Shemiazaz."

"I made them bring me," Pat said, trying to look brave. "I can't just watch my friends march into danger without me, and you needed the people."

Jackson regarded him for a long while. "Do you really mean to help us?"

"This isn't my first experience with a demon. When Jacob took me, it was Ginny and Aiden who saved me. And Tali who protected me after. I owe a lot to you guys."

"Then we will speak more. Our brothers, the Keepers, are always looking for people to recruit, people who know the real dangers we face. The dangers you have now seen and survived. Come find me back at the house. Bring Redeemer. Aiden, you keep an eye on it regardless."

"He means the sword," Aiden leaned over to whisper to Pat.

Pat glanced over to where Shemiazaz's body lay, sword protruding from his chest. "The one in that thing?" Pat's voice went high.

Aiden laughed. "He's harmless now."

"Well," Ginny said with a smile, "it looks like you'll be our brother soon."

Pat grinned, looking down.

"I'm so proud of you," Tali said, wrapping her arm around him.

The clean up crews began to arrive, and Aiden looked around him with a sigh. Most of the demons were gone thanks to the heavenfire, but the bodies of the fallen Alliance remained. The dog demons had done most of the damage with their teeth and claws. Several members stood near their friends, tears in their eyes as the crews walked amongst the corpses with body bags.

Aiden breathed deeply. This loss was great, but for the first time in a while, he felt like he could finally relax. Looking around at his friends, he was very grateful. Grateful that he had them, grateful he didn't have to say goodbye to any of them. Grateful the dangers of Jacob and his father were gone from this world forever. He had so much to look forward to now. He squeezed Ginny's hand, marveling at her smile.

Together, they could conquer anything.

About the Author

JK Allen wrote her first story just as soon as she learned how to write and hasn't looked back since. Common writing themes that can be found in her work address identity, everyday magic, and the type of strength and courage that can be found in ordinary people. Her reading tastes are as varied as the genres she enjoys writing, from Jane Austen to Diana Wynne Jones. When she's not writing, you can find her painting, drawing, or lost in the pages of a book. Or on Tik Tok.

Ginny's story continues in the third and final book,

Demonkind

Marta awoke suddenly. Her head throbbed, and she raised a shaky hand to feel the lump that was raised on the back of her head. She groaned, sitting up and wiping the grit of sand from the side of her face. She was on the beach of Lake Locke.

She looked around, heart racing. That wench, Ginny, was taking determined steps towards her Jacob, his dagger in her traitorous hand. He stood facing the cursed Alliance scum with no idea of Ginny's approach. A scream caught in Marta's throat as Ginny lifted the dagger in both hands and thrust it into Jacob's back, up to the hilt. His face registered shock, then pain before he collapsed. Ginny followed suit.

And just like that, he was gone. From this realm at least. It should have been impossible. After all, Ginny's blood was protecting him. But Ginny had closed the lake portal and now this. Her precious Jacob's mortal form was dead. Her heart wrenched in her chest. And her stomach lurched. But as much as she wanted to fall to pieces here, she couldn't remain.

Jacob would remain a demon in perdition, but that was no place for the man she had raised and guided for the last 90 years. Jacob had been a half-demon, and a powerful one at that. His father, the first of the greater demons, had the child to find what was needed to free him from the chains that kept him in eternal darkness in Perdition. Marta had been Shemiazaz's servant for a long time before Jacob was born, but for decades now, it had been her and Jacob.

And he was meant to rule on Earth. She had to get him back. And soon.

Shemiazaz had finally been freed from his chains and was battling the angel Grace in the sky above the Alliance fight. She had once been Alliance, the angelborn who protected the worthless humans from demonkind, but she had burned that bridge when she joined Shemiazaz, becoming a changeling instead. She lived off demon blood, and it made her strong—she never aged, and she healed from all her wounds. Accursedly not in time to keep Jacob alive.

Now Jacob's father was shot from the sky by a lightning strike, curving away from them all as Grace landed near his daughter, Ginny. Marta could waste no time getting away from this accursed beach. She knew Shemiazaz did not care for his son and would be no help in getting Jacob back, so she had no use for him. She grabbed her pack, which contained the three precious Eternal Tomes Jacob had stolen for her, and scrambled backwards. When she was sure no one was watching her, she ran, fleeing into the dark, faster than mortal eyes could fathom.

The tomes were books given to men from the angel called Grace. They contained sigils and rituals in the Angelic Tongue that worked like magic, bringing clay to life or transporting someone anywhere in the world. She stopped now to use this last sigil, drawing it on the ground in her blood, slicing the side of her finger to write. A black haze of light shot up, and she stepped into it, concentrating on where she wanted to go. Their safe house they had prepared if anything happened to them. Now the worst had happened, and Marta was alone. Again.

Her eyes were hot with unspent tears as she entered the gloom of the safe house. It was bleak after the resplendent comfort of the lake house and resoundingly empty without Jacob. But she would get the Alliance back; get her revenge once again. She recalled the first time she had triumphed over them with a strained grin. The night she became a changeling and changed her destiny, wresting control of her life back into her own hands.

She was sixteen again and back in the Alliance house in New York. The skies were overcast and a dismal grey outside the large picturesque windows of the library. Mikal stood before her, his blue eyes tired and sad.

"Let me see them," Marta screamed again, running frantic fingers through her bedraggled hair.

Mikal paused, rubbing his forehead as he watched her. "They are being taken care of."

Marta turned her back on him and began pacing the room. "By James? You are wrong. He cannot help them, will not. The healing sigil can, and you know this."

"They can't get the healing sigil, they are not angelborn. And James is our best healer."

Marta turned on him, eyes flashing. "I am best healer you have." Her voice thickened and her Eastern European accent grew heavier under the stress she felt.

"That is your pride talking. You are still learning."

"They die." She swallowed hard. "And all because I joined you stupid Alliance. Angelborn is useless in real world. I cannot even save my family. What good does Alliance do me?"

"They would have found you, either way. Demons always find our kind."

"Papa, Veruka, Vanya, I did this to you. I killed you." Sheing wailed before turn murderous eyes on Mikal. "No, they are dead because of you!"

"You don't know that," he started, but stopped when he saw Sophia approaching them with a downcast expression.

Marta knew they were gone then with a harrowing finality. She howled like a wounded animal, clutching her sides. She sobbed like that for a few minutes before rearing up, wild-eyed.

"You will pay for this."

She raked her nails across Mikal's face before turning to flee the room. Sophia jumped out of the way, then rushed to Mikal.

"What will she do?" Sophia asked the retreating figure of Marta.

"God help us."

Marta couldn't go back to her family's house. It hurt too much to see the empty chairs and beds that would never be filled again. And the Alliance would look for her there. She slept wherever she could, washing when she could in public bathrooms. She was not the only nameless shadow in the city. She was biding her time until she could steal what she needed for her plan to work. She would avenge her family by destroying the Alliance any way she could. The dreams were her answer. She would make her dreams come true.

When the next Alliance meeting was just about to start, Marta watched the house. Security was always lax, but tonight every single member would be conveniently in the same place, giving Marta access to the rest of the house. The rest would be like shooting fish in a barrel, as the Americans would say.

She climbed the tree next to the house and sidled down a branch and into the library's open window. She had seen these different rituals before while studying as a healer. James always kept secret copies of the Eternal Tomes that would allow her to do great things. She had learned where he hid them, in a secret panel behind his desk. He only had the one tome, the Book of Rituals, but it would be enough. She had learned the last sigil she needed to avenge her family, may they be resting. Shemiazaz had shown her in her dream last night.

She found the summoning spell in the tome and got to work carving a pentagram into the floor. She worked feverishly but in silence, not wanting anyone to interrupt her. She wrote the name of the greater demon in her blood, just as she had been instructed to in her last dream. Then she quietly began chanting.

The air grew hotter and loose paper swirled from James's desk, as if a desert wind blew across the room. The sigil flashed and burned into the floor and a shadowy figure rose out of it, cloaked in heavy, black chains. Shemiazaz was the first demon transformed from an angel for all his sins. As punishment, he was trapped in perdition by those very chains to remain until the end of days when judgment would come for all.

His skin was a pallid grey, with scales crawling down his neck to the leathery black wings on his back. He grinned at her and licked his lips. "You wish for vengeance."

"Yes." Marta trembled with anticipation.

"It will require me to take more of your life force from you."

"Kill me, but punish them first."

The demon's eyes glittered, and he smiled again.

Marta felt a sharp pain in her core as Shemiazaz breathed in and grew more substantial and corporeal. The pain was intense, and she could hardly see, her eyes blearing and unfocusing, but the shape of the demon had disappeared. The yanking on her center being pulled towards the center of the house.

She felt another pull and screamed. Trembling on the floor, she thought this was death, and she could hardly lift her head when Shemiazaz reappeared in a flash. He looked triumphant.

"It is done. Every last person in this house is dead."

"Thank you." Tears leaked from the corners of her eyes, and she sat up shakily.

Shemiazaz beckoned her closer. She crawled to his feet.

"Before I must leave, I will reward you for summoning me." Shemiazaz used a long black talon to slit his wrist. "Drink, and live forever."

Marta was too tired to do anything but comply without a thought to the consequences. He had helped her achieve her ends, what was damning her soul after losing everything? The blood burned as it coursed through her body, and she gave way to spasms as she felt it cut its way through her, opening her up. She bit down on her screams for the second time that evening.

Then, everything calmed and she heard the soft sound of her breathing, but also her own steady heartbeat. All pain had been erased and her senses sharpened so that she could see and hear everything with a painful clarity.

"You are mine now. Together we will bring about the end of the entire Alliance, not just one chapter. Take these vials, you will need my blood to stay alive, but you will never again know weakness. You will never get sick, your wounds will regenerate, and you will not age beyond what you have tonight. But there was nothing to be done about that.”

“What you mean?” Marta asked, breathing faster and clutching her cheek in her hand.

“You have aged tonight when I used your life force to exact your revenge.”

“Aged? How old?”

“You are now the same as a forty-year-old woman.”

Marta closed her eyes, but nodded. Her youth was gone but it was a small price to pay.

“I give you a mighty gift today.”

“Thank you, master. I am but your servant.”

Shemiazaz stood in the pentagram with a bitter expression. He began to fade, becoming like smoke once more before disappearing down into the sigil. Marta finally stood, feeling her newfound strength pulse through her. She thrummed with a feeling of vitality. She visited every room in the house, taking money, clothes, anything she desired and gloating over the bodies. She heard the others coming towards the house long before they could reach her. With a last look, she tore out of the house, moving so fast she was nothing more than a shadowy blur in the night, moving too fast for human eyes to track.

She had once been Alliance, descendants of the angel Grace who had come into contact with demons and had their powers activated. Her family had not been recruited when she was, and they had paid the ultimate price. She had thought that joining the Alliance would keep them all safe after her experience with a demon and knowing how deadly they were. How wrong she had been. The Alliance had betrayed her, so she’d pledged herself to Jacob’s father. Then his son. She had been unable to do anything else. But everyone she cared for died. She had to get him back. The tomes would hold the answer. She knew it, she just needed time to find it.

Not wishing for harsh light, Marta lit a candle and walked brusquely to her cramped room. It hardly fit more than a bed, but that was all she needed. A place to sit and study the tomes. She settled on the creaky bed and pulled out the newest one they had acquired, the Book of Infernal Rituals. The lake portal was closed. She needed to find another way to bring Jacob back to the mortal realm.

Marta.

The voice of Shemiazaz echoed through her mind. She steeled herself against him. She was angelborn, one of the few strong enough to do so, though it drained her. He cared nothing for his son, so she cared nothing for helping him. He could reach into the mind of any man and manipulate them to his will. He had no need of her.

She opened the book, preparing for the longest night of her life.